The RABBIT'S GIFT

THE RABBIT'S GIFT

JESSICA VITALIS

Greenwillow Books
An Imprint of HarperCollins*Publishers*

The Rabbit's Gift
Copyright © 2022 by Jessica Vitalis

The text of this book is set in 13-point Granjon.
Book design by Paul Zakris

Library of Congress Cataloging-in-Publication Data

Names: Vitalis, Jessica, author.
Title: The rabbit's gift / Jessica Vitalis.
Description: First edition. |
New York : Greenwillow Books, an imprint of HarperCollins Publishers, [2022] |
Audience: Ages Ages 8-12. | Audience: Grades 4-6. |
Summary: When the delicate balance between the mythical rabbits and the people of Montpeyroux breaks down, runt Quincy and twelve-year-old Fleurine learn to trust each other to ensure their respective communities' survival.
Identifiers: LCCN 2022019436 | ISBN 9780063067462 (hardback) |
ISBN 9780063067486 (ebook)
Subjects: CYAC: Rabbits—Fiction. | Magic—Fiction. | Trust—Fiction. | Fantasy. |
LCGFT: Novels.
Classification: LCC PZ7.1.V595 Rab 2022 | DDC [Fic]—dc23
LC record available at https://lccn.loc.gov/2022019436

22 23 24 25 26 PC/LSCH 10 9 8 7 6 5 4 3 2 1
First Edition

GREENWILLOW BOOKS

*To the old lady who lives in the desert
with metal in her knees*

I used to believe . . .

that every story had a hero and a villain. Take this story, for example. There was a time when I would have insisted that the hero was me, Quincy Rabbit. Not that you'd know it by looking at me—I'm no Angora Rex or anything like that. But I am the one who saved the Warren (not to mention the future of Montpeyroux). If that's not heroic, I don't know what is.

The problem is that I'm also the one who started the trouble in the first place.

That's not to say it was *all* my fault. I had plenty of help. Not from a rabbit—from a human. A human named Fleurine d'Aubigné.[1]

---

1. *Humans have the strangest names. This one is pronounced Floor-EEN Doo-bin-YAY.*

Once, I would have told you that she was the villain in this story. A stubborn, selfish, thoughtless villain. And I would have been partly right. But I would have been partly wrong, too. Because I've learned that sometimes the only difference between a hero and a villain is which side you're on.

Chapter One: *Quincy*

I'm getting ahead of myself. Let's go back to the days before I thought much about heroes and villains, to the days before I encountered the human world, to the days before I ever heard the name Fleurine d'Aubigné.

In fact, let's go back to the morning Maman rose early to sort carrots at the far end of the burrow, waking me from a restless slumber. This story begins the moment I pulled myself from the heap of tangled limbs belonging to my eleven brothers and sisters and hopped to her side, taking care not to stumble in the dim morning light trickling in from the burrow's only entrance.

"Good morning, greetings, good day," I said.

"Good morning, greetings, good day," Maman

answered, gently pressing her sable forehead against mine, resting it on the white stripe that started at my nose and ran the length of my otherwise black body.

"Can I help?" I asked.

Maman twisted to lick at the graying fur on her arthritic hind leg and then continued taking inventory. "I'm working on breakfast. Why don't you rouse the others? The Chou are waiting."

My ears drooped at the mention of the long day to come. Maman always claimed that farming was honorable, that we were created by Great Maman Rabbit to be the stewards of human life, but I didn't want to be stuck in the Warren forever. If only the Committee would assign me to transport duty, I'd be able to get out and see the world.

I dreamed of crisscrossing the country in the complex system of underground tunnels I'd heard about but never seen, transplanting Chou de vie, and returning with the purple carrots we needed to survive. I imagined my siblings hunched at my feet, looking up at me with awe as I shared strange and wonderful stories filled with daring and intrigue. But my twelfth birthday had come and gone, and I was no closer to being assigned to transport than I had been the year before.

Perhaps next year, the Committee said.

You could still have a growth spurt, Maman said.

What a bunch of rotten carrots! Sure, I was a runt, but I could manage a Chou de vie. (Chou are the cabbage-like plants we grow here in the Warren. Transport rabbits dig them up and deliver them to humans, who peel back the velvety purple leaves to find a human baby nestled inside.)

Besides, what I lacked in size and strength, I more than made up for with my intelligence. Not to brag or anything, but I could calculate how many Chou we had planted faster than any other rabbit. And I was better than the Committee at keeping track of which rabbits were assigned to which tasks. Plus, I never forgot a single fact I ever heard.

So what if I occasionally made small errors? I mean yes, it could have ended poorly when I misjudged the depth of the water in the creek, but we pulled Sophie out before any real harm was done. As for mistaking the feathery greens of tempest's lace for purple carrot greens when we were out foraging, anybody might have made the same error. (Anybody who'd never mixed them up and suffered a week of diarrhea, that is. How was I supposed to know purple carrots never grew in the wild?)

The truth of the matter was that nothing could happen in the human world that I couldn't handle, if only the Committee would give me a chance. I nosed one of my siblings, a foul mood settling over me like a swarm of pesky mosquitoes.

"Ten more twitches," Sophie mumbled as she rolled over and covered her eyes with her snow-white paws. She was from the last of Maman's litters. Maybe it was because she was a runt like me, or maybe it was her sweet temperament, but I'd always had a soft spot for her.

I couldn't resist tickling her stomach until her giggles signaled she was awake. Then I poked and prodded the rest of the pile. The kits stretched and grumbled and did their best to ignore me.

"Leave me alone, cabbage-breath," Durrell mumbled. He rolled over, releasing a cloud of mysterious scents from the human world (the smells clung to his fur no matter how much he groomed). He'd always been difficult, but after being assigned to transport two seasons earlier than normal, he'd become unbearable.

"Go away or I'll thump you good," Estelle said, stretching her heavily muscled limbs.

Her bad moods were limited to the few minutes between waking up and eating breakfast, but I couldn't really blame her or Durrell for their attitudes. I'd be grumpy, too, if I had to wake up so soon after going to sleep—even if I knew I'd get to go back to bed shortly after. (Maman was a stickler for family meals and insisted they join us even after they were up all night making deliveries—not that they could sleep through our ruckus anyway.)

I hopped to the other side of the pile, but I didn't have any better luck over there.

"Rise and shine," I finally called. "Last one up gets the smallest carrot."

That did the trick. My siblings scrambled to right themselves. They groomed as they waited for breakfast, smoothing their fur and licking their paws to wipe their faces. Maman had pulled a small pile of purple carrots from the stock we stored between the roots of the mighty chestnut tree that stretched over our burrow. My ears swiveled, betraying my agitation. "We're four carrots short," I whispered.

She leaned up against one of the burrow's hard-packed walls. "We'll have to make do with half a carrot each."

The seed of anger that had been germinating[2] in my stomach over the last several months grew taller. Our food shortages were all the humans' fault. Well, not *all* the humans' fault. It's possible that I might have occasionally snuck an extra carrot or two (or three), hoping the nutrients would initiate a growth spurt.

Guilt cropped up alongside my anger, making me cringe. I'd known our supply was dwindling. But I hadn't let myself believe the Committee, much less Great Maman Rabbit, would let things get this bad. Now I counted the meager stock from which Maman had pulled breakfast. If something didn't change dramatically, we'd be stuck on this half-carrot diet forever.

What if the supply continues to drop? I shushed the

---

2. *Maman says I have the vocabulary of a rabbit five times my age. I'll try to keep things simple for you, if I can.*

voice in my head, unable to imagine how we'd survive on a quarter carrot each.

I reared upright, stuffed this morning's carrots in my stomach pouch, and began doling out one to each pair of my siblings. (If you know anything about rabbit breeds, you must already know that Angora Roux have pouches—how else are we to transport the Chou?)

Durrell pulled himself upright, towering over me and showing off the naturally muscled hind legs that had grown even stronger after he was assigned to transport. "Who made you the carrot boss?"

Usually, his snarky comments didn't ruffle my fur. I always helped Maman when I could, hoping to prove my worth. Today, Durrell's comment stung. I wasn't the carrot boss. I was more like a carrot *thief.*

I wished I could challenge him. But I'd only spent a few minutes on my back legs and they were already quivering.

"Don't let him bother you," Sophie whispered.

I tucked my head and moved on, leaving behind Durrell's grumbling about our skimpy meal and how it was high time we went on strike. No one was more unhappy with the humans than I was, but without a way to communicate with them, a strike wouldn't do any good.

We crunched our way through breakfast, ignoring Claire's complaints that Bella wasn't sharing the greens and crowding around Victor to ooh and ah when he announced he had a loose tooth.

"I'm still hungry," Estelle said after we finished eating.

Cries of "me too" filled the burrow.

Maman sighed. "We'll have to forage."

I groaned right along with my siblings. Foraging meant leaving the safety of the Warren. (Transport duty isn't without its dangers, but most of that time is spent in the tunnels. Lingering in the open is an invitation for trouble.) Foraging also meant upset stomachs all around. We could technically eat clover and some of the vegetation outside the Warren, but none of it settled well. Besides, nothing we found in the forest matched the nutritional value of the purple carrots we needed to thrive. Not that there was any choice—my ribs practically poked through my coat.

"Out we go," Maman said. "Let's be quick about it.

The Chou won't grow themselves."

We grumbled under our breath as we filed outside. Though the sun was already overhead and the transport rabbits reported an extreme heat spell across the country, temperatures inside the Warren stayed temperate year-round. Hundreds of rows of Chou stretched out in front of us, dotting the landscape in colors ranging from the lichen green of the baby sprouts to the dark purple of the Chou ready for harvest.

Other rabbits emerged from the dozens of burrows circling the field. Where we normally called out cheerful salutations as we made our way to our workstations, today we greeted each other with frightened nods as we swallowed our smattering of cecotropes[3] and hopped toward the Warren's exit. The normally sweet, slightly milky Chou-scented air was tinged with the rank smell of fear.

Our foraging often attracted predators. Despite the Warren's healing magic, all of us had lost loved ones. Our burrow was no exception—we lost Papá and

---

3. *Normally these soft droppings are like rabbit vitamins. But without enough carrots in our bellies, we weren't producing enough to make a difference.*

Grand-Maman to the dangers in the woods. (Maman claims that Grand-Papá died of old age, but I heard her telling a friend that he died of a broken heart after losing Grand-Maman.)

If only we were still the size of the Angora Rex. They could deliver ten Chou in a single night without breaking a sweat. They were so big and strong that when the ground cracked open, a Rex stretched herself across the gap, holding it together until Great Maman Rabbit could mend it. Another time, it rained for so many days and nights that an Angora Rex stuck one pair of every animal in the country in her pouch and floated until things dried out.

Then again, the carrots the Rex ate were the size of a human's arm. That was before the plague that wiped out all the giant carrots and the Angora Rex along with them, leaving only a few crops of puny carrots behind. The Committee claimed this forced Great Maman Rabbit to create us, but I wasn't so sure. If Great Maman Rabbit was that powerful, then why didn't she save the Rex—or the carrots—in the first place?

Even if it was true, she obviously didn't count on

the greedy humans starving us to death.

Maman said they probably weren't doing it on purpose, but I found that hard to believe, too. They might not have been able to control the larger carrots disappearing, but they could definitely add more of the smaller carrots to each bundle. Or ask for more children. Either one would go a long way toward solving our problems.

I shook my head, realizing it was in the clouds again. Maman said I had to learn to focus on the tasks at hand.

I followed my siblings through the shimmering air between two massive evergreens.

Everything outside the Warren felt different. It was more than the sweltering heat. More than the stark colors of the flowers dotting the meadow. More than the crunch of the unseen animals treading on the pine-scented needles that had fallen in the forest surrounding the meadow. The entire world was sharper. More foreboding. Less magic. My whiskers twitched and my stomach twisted.

Stop with the collywobbles,[4] I lectured myself.

---

4. *I'm prone to stomachaches when I'm anxious or scared.*

Maman was forever telling me not to let my imagination run away. Right now, I needed to keep my wits about me. Focus on filling first my belly, then my pouch, and getting back to the Warren.

Maman stood guard at the Warren's entrance, keeping watch for predators. The heat had crisped much of the clover, making it dry and crunchy and even less suitable for eating than usual. Durrell, Estelle, and the rest of the transport rabbits quickly claimed the few green patches nearby, forcing the rest of us to spread out.

Within moments, the whole of the meadow had been taken over. I scanned the clearing and finally spotted a small patch of greens all the way on the other side. I hated to venture that far from the Warren's entrance, but my stomach insisted.

Fear forced me to eat at twice my normal pace. Still, I took care not to nibble so much as a whisker's worth of the tempest's lace that grew among the clover.

My ears swiveled, constantly monitoring for danger. Every rustle of leaves could be a bear's or wolf's approach. Or the hawk that had plagued us all summer. A dozen times, I nearly bolted for the Warren.

The sun beat down on my back. Sweat pooled in my mouth, causing me to drool in a most unappealing manner.

My bitter thoughts returned. We shouldn't have to spend all our time and energy growing Chou for the humans—we should be growing carrots for ourselves. When I brought up the idea of getting our paws on some purple carrot seeds, the Committee only thanked me and sent me on my way. (To be fair, they also said they couldn't risk upsetting the natural balance and that they'd asked Great Maman Rabbit for guidance. But it was clear they had no intention of entertaining my suggestion. Why do they think you have to be old and gray to have good ideas?)

No matter. The idea *was* a good one, and I was going to see it through, as soon as I figured out how.

Maman rapidly thumped her hind foot, warning us of danger.

Pandemonium broke out as rabbits lunged toward the Warren. My heart thump, thump, thumped in my chest.

I scanned the deep blue sky, then the tree line. A large red fox slunk from trunk to trunk.

My nose twitched. My legs trembled. Even moving at top speed, I'd never make it back to the Warren in time. There weren't any bushes or holes nearby to hide in. Foxes didn't usually go after full-grown Angora Roux, but even at twelve seasons, I was less than half grown.

That's when I noticed Sophie.

Sweet Sophie.

Tired, hot, hungry Sophie. Small enough that a fox wouldn't hesitate to attack. Instead of fleeing, she huddled frozen in fear. Her bright white coat stood out in the crunchy brown grass.

"Sophie!" I yelled.

The fox darted toward her. Its mouth opened, anticipating her neck.

A large stick rested between Sophie and the fox. That was it—my only chance to save her. I gathered my strength. Jumped.

The forest fell silent.

The fox's sharp teeth glinted in the sunlight.

Sophie's wide eyes shined with fear.

The same eyes she'd refused to open that very morning. The same eyes that shined softly as she begged me to play Hop Skip with her. The same eyes that filled with laughter when Marcel told a joke or with tears when a wasp stung the tip of her nose.

I came down on the stick, snapping the world back into motion. The other end flew up, catching the fox in the chin. THWAP!

The fox yelped as its head jerked back, slowing its momentum.

A blur came out of nowhere.

Durrell stood on his hind legs and boxed the fox with his front legs, one quick strike after another.

The fox tucked its tail and ran for the woods.

"That's right," Durrell shouted. "You get out of here and don't come back." He executed a series of adrenaline-filled binkies, flipping and twisting his body every which way. (We might be a special breed created by Great Maman Rabbit to raise and deliver Chou, but that doesn't mean we don't still act like rabbits.)

"Come on," Maman cried from the Warren's entrance. "Get your tails in here."

Durrell nosed Sophie, who didn't utter so much as a squeak as she crossed the meadow. He stuck close to one side of her. I hopped along on the other, shaking at the thought of how close we'd come to losing her.

Inside the Warren, rabbits gathered around us. "Holy cottontails," someone shouted. "That was close!"

"You saved her," another rabbit said. "Way to show that fox what's what!"

Now that I was safely inside the Warren, some of my fear started to melt away. My ears stood tall and proud. I'd saved Sophie. Without me, Durrell wouldn't have caught up in time.

Maman burst into the circle. "What were you thinking, hopping so far from the Warren?" She rested her forehead against Sophie's. "I don't know what I would have done if I'd lost you."

"I'm fine, Maman," Sophie said. "Durrell saved me!"

She pressed up against him. "You're my hero!"

"It was nothing," Durrell said, swelling to about ten times his normal size.

"Hey, I helped, too," I said.

"Thanks for trying, Quincy," Sophie said.

For trying? TRYING?

My ears lay back against my head. Chaos broke out as the rest of the rabbits began talking, sharing what they witnessed and asking Durrell to replay the whole thing in slow motion.

Nobody cared that I'd slowed the fox down. That without me, Sophie would have been fox food before Durrell reached her. I backed through the crowd, hoping someone would notice.

I was outside the cluster when Maman called for calm. (Even though her ears aren't big enough for her to be a Committee member, every rabbit in the Warren knows when she gives an order, they'd better listen.)

"That's quite enough excitement for one day," she said. "Let's deliver breakfast to the Committee and get to work."

I dug in my pouch for clover before remembering I'd been so busy stuffing my face that I hadn't harvested any before the fox attacked. I ducked my head, hoping Maman wouldn't notice. As she collected what the other rabbits had gathered, my stomach lurched, already complaining about the horrible menu.

It's your fault we're hungry in the first place, the

unwelcome voice whispered in the back of my mind. I tried to swat the words away, but there was no denying the truth. The carrot shortage wasn't my fault, but if I hadn't eaten more than my fair share, there would be more to go around.

"My stomach hurts," Sophie said. "Can I take the day off?"

Several of my siblings groaned in agreement.

Maman licked Sophie's cheek. "I'm sorry," she said. "The Warren will soon set your stomachs right, but the Chou won't wait. Now, does anyone else have clover?"

Her gaze fell on me. I busied myself cleaning a paw. She sighed. "Very well, then. Get to work."

My stomach twisted again, and I felt a familiar flash of resentment. It didn't make sense to spend all our time farming Chou. Just because the Committee didn't like the idea of adding a crop of purple carrots didn't mean it wouldn't work.

Sophie's words replayed in my head. *Thanks for trying, Quincy.*

If I was ever going to get her—or any rabbit in the Warren—to respect me, I was going to have to prove myself. Do something no one else had done.

An idea took shape in my mind.

In order to pull it off, I'd need purple carrot seeds—seeds that only the humans had.

I gulped. Sneaking into the human world would mean leaving the Warren without permission, which was strictly forbidden. And more than a little dangerous.

But I had to save us, even if it meant breaking a rule or two along the way.

Chapter Two: *Quincy*

Maman would never agree to my quest, so I had no choice but to spend the day farming as I waited for the cover of dark in order to slip away. Over the centuries, we'd perfected our production techniques, which involved assigning duties on a weekly basis. Besides transport, weeding was the only job that rarely changed. It was reserved for the youngest of kits. (Their palates weren't yet refined, allowing them to tolerate the bitter taste of the weeds prone to sprouting up around the Chou.)

The rest of us rotated between washing, planting, hydrating, and fertilizing (an exacting process that depended on how fast we needed each plant to ripen, determined by Great Maman Rabbit in accordance with human demand). At least this week I was assigned to a task I enjoyed: washing the seeds to prepare them for planting.

Transport rabbits rotated between delivering Chou and collecting dirty soul seeds from the ashes dumped into the tunnel below the humans' crematoriums. (This particular job, while still more prestigious than any here at the Warren, isn't a favorite—the rabbits on duty always return covered in soot.)

Today's pile of seeds wasn't particularly large, but still, it took the better part of the day to wash, dry, and rewash them. Most rabbits hated this task. They had to repeatedly drop the pebble-sized seeds in a shallow, water-filled basin on the edge of a small brook and then pull them out again, soaking their faces and staining their fur with the colors flowing from the seeds.

I never had to worry about that on account of my black fur. (Angora Roux are generally known for their brown or white fur. I wasn't the only black rabbit in the Warren, but I was the only one with the coloring of an animal Durrell called a skunk. I wasn't sure whether or not he was pulling my leg because there wasn't any such animal in Montpeyroux, but he swore some of the wealthier humans brought them in from another country and kept them as pets. He also said they were known for their terrible smell.)

As far as I was concerned, spending the day drenched was a small price to pay for the chance to admire the colors the memories made as they bled into the cool brook. Some were soft and pastel, like the evening sky. Others were as bright as the birds in the trees. Occasionally, a seed bled nothing but a murky grayish-brown into the otherwise crystal-clear water. Those seeds always made me shudder. I couldn't begin to imagine what awful lives those humans must have lived.

Today, time crept along at a caterpillar's pace. My impatience prevented me from taking pleasure in the myriad[5] of colors swirling in the water.

Midafternoon, I looked up to find the head of the Committee hopping toward me.

A surprise inspection. My stomach had only started to settle from the morning's clover. Now it twisted again from nerves or irritation—I wasn't sure which.

"Good afternoon, greetings, good day," Chesney said. According to Maman, his coat was once black,

---

5. *This word is way more interesting than variety, don't you think?*

but it had been gray for as long as I could remember. Cataracts clouded his marbled eyes. In addition to being one of the oldest rabbits in the Warren, he had the biggest ears, so he could hear Great Maman Rabbit's instructions on how many Chou to ready for transplanting, and when and where to deliver them, better than anyone else.

"Good afternoon, greetings, good day," I said, settling back on my haunches and perking my small ears in the hopes that they'd appear bigger than they really were.

While Chesney nuzzled my stack of already-washed seeds, I hardly dared breathe. If any other rabbit missed a speck of color, Chesney would simply send the seed back for another washing. But when I made a mistake, he acted as though I'd let the entire Warren down.

He separated one seed from the stack. My whiskers quivered.

"Do you see that?" he asked.

A faint bit of red glistened on the tip of the white seed. "I'll wash it again," I said, hating how meek my voice sounded.

"Wash them all again."

"Every one of them?" I squeaked.

"Every one. Quincy, I don't need to tell you how important—"

While he continued on about how special we were, about how Great Maman Rabbit had honored the Angora Roux with the sole responsibility for human life, about how tragic it would be for them to be born with part of another soul, I focused on calculating how many hours until I could escape. Until I could prove to him—to the whole Warren—that I deserved their respect.

Sudden silence made me realize I'd missed something.

"Pardon?"

Chesney sighed. "How many Chou do we have planted?"

My whiskers quivered with annoyance. They asked the same questions every time, as if hoping I'd eventually mess up. "Nine thousand, seven hundred and sixteen."

We normally had around eighty-four hundred Chou in the field, but with the drop in human demand, supply had been building. In theory, the growing size of the crop didn't matter since the ripening process didn't commence until we received orders from Great Maman Rabbit. (No, I'm not going to get into specifics—sharing my story is one thing, divulging the secrets of our Warren is something else. Suffice it to say that we initiate a pre-ripening before the transport rabbits deliver the Chou to specially built planters in the front of the humans' homes. The rabbits leave behind a final ripening agent, ensuring that the baby will be ready for harvest shortly thereafter.)

Still, I'd calculated that each Chou remained in the ground an average of ninety days. I wondered what would happen if we reached a point where they'd have to grow a lot longer. (We plant every seed the day after it comes in so that it doesn't dry out and die.)

"If we deliver eighty-seven Chou tonight, how many will there be?"

The half carrot I had for breakfast turned to a stone in my stomach. We used to average a hundred deliveries a night. Lately, it'd dropped down to ninety-five. Now eighty-seven? That might not sound like much, but losing out on sixty-five carrots a night added up fast when it came to feeding every rabbit in the Warren five meals a day.

"We're really going to starve if this keeps up," I said.

"It's not for us to question Great Maman Rabbit," Chesney said. "How many?"

I forced myself to swallow my frustration and mumbled, "Nine thousand, six hundred and twenty-nine."

"And if we plant one hundred and three seeds today?"

"Nine thousand, seven hundred and thirty-two."

He asked me a few more questions and then hopped on.

Maman said the Committee was always quizzing me because they saw my potential, but I knew better. The quizzes were only an excuse—if I wasn't always messing up, they wouldn't have to keep a closer-than-usual eye on me.

Finally, the sun dropped behind the trees, and we retired to our burrows. Dinner was another half carrot, but I was so nervous about my upcoming departure that I could hardly choke it down. My siblings complained about the lack of food, but Maman was still shaken from this morning's near miss and refused to let us out to forage.

"An empty stomach is better than a dead rabbit," she said. (I personally thought this was a little harsh, but nobody asked my opinion.)

While we licked our paws clean, I tried to commit each of my brothers' and sisters' faces to memory. Leaving the Warren was no small thing—I didn't know for sure when, or even if, I'd ever return. But this was something I had to do. If I succeeded, the risk would be well worth it. If I didn't, well, no one ever became a hero by sitting around worrying about failure.

I hoped everyone would fall asleep without much fuss, but Sophie pestered Maman for a bedtime story. I hid my frustration by focusing on my evening grooming ritual, which consisted of licking my paws and swiping them across my nose and eyes.

Maman told a familiar favorite—the time a brown bear cub fell out of a tree and injured its paw. It was about to be eaten by a wolf when an Angora Rex intervened, tucking the cub in its pouch and carrying it back to its cave.

As the story went on, I realized it wasn't such a bad

idea—at least it was something to help pass the time. I couldn't leave until much later in the night anyway, when I was sure all the transport rabbits had already left the Warren. The last thing I wanted was to run into one of them and have to explain myself.

After the story, I took care to remain on the edge of the furry mess of warm bodies, frustrated by my siblings, who tossed and turned late into the night. (If you've ever had to fall asleep with an empty stomach, you'll understand. The bite of hunger is hard to ignore.)

Finally, the transport rabbits left to report for their shifts, and the burrow filled with gentle snores and twitching limbs. Twice, Sophie cried out, undoubtedly reliving her brush with the fox.

After she settled, I deemed it safe to leave. But sneaking up on a rabbit—or in this case sneaking away from a sleeping pile of rabbits—is no easy thing. (Not only are our eyes set on the sides of our heads so that we have nearly three-hundred-and-sixty-degree vision, but we also have a clear eyelid that allows us to sleep with our eyes open so we can constantly scan for danger.)

In order to pull it off, I had to inch out of the

burrow slowly, making small movements over time so as not to attract anyone's attention.

The Rabbit in the Moon smiled gently from high above, bathing me in warm light as I emerged into the tepid night air. Hopping as softly as I could manage, I cut across the field, eager to reach the Warren's exit before the watch rabbit noticed me. Although Maman occasionally let us leave the burrow to gaze at the stars or play Fox and Rabbit under the cover of dark, I'd never been outside by myself. It was strangely liberating, and I barely resisted the urge to binkie as I made my way down a long, straight row of Chou de vie. Chirping crickets serenaded my departure. A light breeze kissed my fur.

My confidence faltered as I approached the evergreens. I crouched under their protective branches, flashing back to the fox's sharp teeth. That predator was still out there somewhere. There was a tunnel entrance inside the Warren, but I couldn't risk running into a lingering transport rabbit or whichever Committee member had stayed up to monitor their safe return.

Perhaps a change of mind was in order. I could

sneak back into the burrow without anyone being the wiser.

I might have done that if my pinched stomach hadn't demanded I continue. After gathering my courage, I hopped between the pines. The meadow's warm, humid air enveloped me. A wolf howled in the distance. I froze, my ears twisting every which way.

Finding no signs of immediate danger, I bounded across the clearing, too nervous to bother stopping for a mouthful of clover. On the other side, I entered the forest and kept moving until I reached a flowering ninebark. When snowdrifts in the meadow had forced us to venture farther from the Warren than we liked to forage, Durrell had bragged that the bush hid a tunnel. My nose twitched. This was well and truly it—the point of no return. I pushed several branches aside and hopped into the dark.

The tunnel wasn't so very different from our burrow, although it smelled more of damp earth than tired bunnies. I let out a long breath. I could do this. I *had* to do this. I began hopping, wondering how I'd ever find the capital. (I didn't know exactly where purple carrots were grown, but I figured that was my best chance.)

After I moved a fair distance from the entrance, it disappeared, creating the appearance of a dead end behind me. I knew it would reopen if I (or any Roux) approached it, but the sudden switch from light to dark was disconcerting, and I couldn't help but feel trapped. I shook off my nerves and continued on. Although I couldn't see, my whiskers kept me from running into the sides of the tunnel.

I reached a cavernous spot that I sensed was a hub. Paths shot off in several different directions. I listened closely. If only my ears weren't as small as the rest of my underdeveloped body, this trip would be a lot easier. The indistinct murmuring of what I thought might be human voices came from one direction. From another, the neighing of what had to be a horse. I sniffed. Pondered.

The faint scent of carrots sweetened nearly every path. Finally, I realized the tunnel with the loudest noise also had the strongest carrot scent—I could only hope that, as the capital, Mignon would have the most of both. In any case, standing around in the dark didn't accomplish anything.

A short time later, I took a wrong turn. After several

twitches, the smell of carrots grew faint. I retraced my path until I was back on Mignon's scent-trail. It wasn't long before my legs grew shaky, but I passed the hours by replaying the fox's attack and reliving the moments after, when my brothers and sisters crowded around Durrell in awe. I imagined the enthusiastic greeting I'd receive when I returned with an entire pouch of purple carrot seeds. Finally, I'd be the hero.

Instead of telling stories of the Angora Rex that had once ruled these woods, my siblings' heads would be filled with my bravery, my daring. Their stomachs would be full, too. I remembered their grumblings after they'd gotten half a carrot at breakfast. A rush of bitterness washed over me, replacing my optimism. *Stupid humans.* According to the transport rabbits, more and more humans were leaving the countryside and crowding into towns and cities. It wasn't right that they weren't using all the extra land to grow more carrots.

I was so lost in my thoughts that I didn't hear another rabbit approaching until it was too late.

"Good evening, greetings, good night," a transport rabbit called.

I jumped, then froze. (Most animals have a fight

or flight response. Rabbits have a freeze and flee response.)

In order to avoid drawing suspicion, I was going to have to say something. "Good ev—" I stopped myself and tried again, this time attempting to deepen my voice to sound more like Durrell. "Good evening, greetings, good night."

"Durrell, is that you?"

I barely held back a groan. Just my luck, running into Estelle.

"Yep," I said. "It's me. Durrell. Your brother." *Stop talking already!*

"You sound funny," Estelle said.

"Coming down with a bit of a cold, maybe."

"You'd better hurry and get back to the Warren. But I thought you had a delivery in Toulouse. What are you doing on your way to Mignon?"

"Oh, um—" I scrambled for an excuse. "I finished so quickly that they sent me out again."

Estelle responded with her usual fire. "They better not try to send me out again after a measly half carrot for dinner."

"This is the last one," I said, hoping I was right.

"Okay, well, happy hopping," Estelle said.

"Happy hopping," I echoed, eager to be on my way (and thrilled to know that I was headed the right direction).

Eventually, thumps and bumps and any number of other unfamiliar sounds flooded my ears. The ground above me seemed to rumble. My breath came in faster puffs. A faint light glinted in the tunnel ahead. I rushed forward, eager to complete my mission.

A flowering ninebark, only slightly larger than the one that had hidden the entrance to the tunnel, marked my exit. The golden light of dawn greeted me. A human structure I was pretty sure was a bridge stretched over me. A gentle creek flowed under it, whispering reminders of home. Maman and my siblings were probably curled up in the burrow, still sound asleep. My heart ached, but I forced myself to hop up a steep slope.

I shivered as I surveyed the scene in front of me. Carefully manicured bushes lined pebbled paths. Unfamiliar smells saturated the air, overwhelming me with their intensity. The clatter and clunk of new sounds added to my disorientation. A starling squawked from a branch overhead, startling me into motion.

Pruned bushes soon gave way to chaotic beds filled with flowers of all sizes, shapes, and colors. Moving quickly, I hopped along until the path opened onto a curious meadow made of smooth, flat stones. I'd heard of a place like this before. I closed my eyes and searched my memory. A *plaza*, Durrell had called it.

A small, still pond sat in the center. (Truthfully, this bothered me more than anything else—our brook was ever moving and changing). Next to the water, a stone structure rose high in the air. I gasped—this had to be made by humans. Rather than tunneling into the earth, they apparently used rocks and trees to assemble above-ground burrows right out in the open. (Maman says they don't have to worry about predators because they're at the top of the food chain.)

Although transport rabbits had described humans plenty of times, I wasn't quite ready for my first encounter. Taking care to steer far away from the building, I hopped to the edge of the pond and lowered my face to drink. After a single sip, I pulled back. The water was murky and stagnant, nothing like the refreshing brook at the Warren.

Regardless, my parched mouth insisted I drink my fill. Once satiated,[6] I continued on my way, letting my ears guide me toward the clamor of human life.

The rocky trail ended at a large stone arch that curved high overhead. A cobblestone street lined with gracious trees stretched out in front of me.

My whiskers twitched anxiously. Enormous homes peeked from between the branches. More than once, Durrell had claimed that humans were magicians. Only magic could explain how they transformed their warrens—cities, he called them—into something so completely different from the surrounding land, something so unnatural.

I'd spent my whole life tucked among my siblings at night, trying to imagine what he might have meant, but nothing could have prepared me for this. Where our Warren felt like part of the surrounding land, everything about this place felt artificial. I shuddered, longing for the comfort of home.

A human hurried down the other side of the street. I gasped. The transport rabbits were right—humans were strange, furless creatures with clipped ears. No

6. *This word is fun because it sounds different than it's spelled: SAY-shee-ate-id.*

wonder they couldn't hear us—not with those tiny nubs!

I pressed myself against a low wall of stacked rocks that seemed designed to keep people out (or was it to keep them in? I couldn't quite tell) and fought to remain calm as the human disappeared down the street. A whiff of something familiar drifted by. Carrots. Right. *Focus*, I reminded myself. I sniffed again. Though the air was thick with the smell of human food and sweat and a million other things I couldn't name, it was also saturated with the sweet smell I was looking for.

The enormous house across the street seemed as good a place to start as any. I perched on the curb, preparing to cross.

A large, four-legged creature with sharp teeth burst from the arch behind me, its hackles raised. A series of deep-chested and exceedingly ferocious barks poured from its mouth. A dog!

It closed the space between us and tightened its muscles, preparing to lunge for my leg.

I sprang into action, zigging and zagging down the block, searching for an opening in the solid rock wall.

The dog followed close behind. I changed tactics and darted across the street, only to find it was guarded by a much taller rock wall. An opening appeared. I ducked inside. The dog's hot breath warmed my tail.

"Hey!"

A human voice shouted behind me. (We speak Montpeyrouxien, although rabbit speech can't be detected by the human ear on account of the tiny nubs I mentioned earlier.)

The dog yelped.

The human seized the dog by the scruff of the neck and dragged it back into the street, lecturing it all the way.

"Get out and stay out," the human shouted as it released its hold on the dog.

With a last, longing glance in my direction, the dog slinked away, its thick tail tucked between its legs.

My heart beat so loudly in my chest that I half-expected it to catch the human's attention, but the human returned to its spot at the wall without so much as a glance my way. I sniffed the air. According to the transport rabbits, female humans had a strong wild onion smell. Since nothing like that came from this one, I concluded it was a male. His upright posture reminded me of Maman when she stood on watch duty while we foraged, though I had trouble imagining this man thumping his foot if danger arose.

I tucked myself into the shadow of a bush and pictured telling my brothers and sisters that I'd been chased by a dog. (We'd lost more than one transport rabbit to their vicious pursuits.)

Escaping doesn't mean I'm out of danger, I reminded myself. As my adrenaline returned to normal, I studied the area around me. A house the size of an entire forest towered overhead. Glistening holes that I guessed were windows stared from its face like all-knowing eyes. I'd never seen anything so ostentatious[7] in all my life. The home was surrounded by a vast expanse of the same type of manicured paths and greenery I'd seen when I first emerged from the tunnels. The faint scent of carrots came from the back of the house.

With a quick look at the man, who still paid me no attention, I followed the smell, hoping to find somewhere safer to catch my breath before I helped myself

---

7. *A fancy word to describe fancy stuff.*

to a meal (and hopefully all the seeds I needed).

I'd just spotted the perfect bush when another home came into view. No, not a home. A shed, maybe. This structure was much smaller, with only a single window staring out at me. Something about it was comforting. Inviting. I sniffed. The carrots!

Unable to resist, I raced toward the shed.

My excitement turned to frustration as I hopped around the building. There was no way for me to get in. I whimpered and tucked myself under another leafy bush.

I only had two choices: find a way into that shed or find another source of carrots. I knew I should probably choose the latter, but as I sat evaluating my options, my latest rush of adrenaline disappeared and exhaustion overtook me. Suddenly, I was too tired to think. To move. Sleep claimed me in one giant gulp.

I startled awake, perplexed by a cacophony of new noises—voices, crunching, hammering, clanging, and countless other sounds. That's right—I was in Mignon, and the city had obviously awoken while I slept. I wasn't sure how much time had passed. Enough that Maman had discovered my absence. I wondered what was happening at the Warren. Guilt flickered as I imagined the pain I was undoubtedly causing Maman. But it would all be worth it when I returned.

Human footsteps crunched the grass nearby. I tensed, wondering if I'd been discovered. The steps passed, giving my muddled senses a chance to marvel at the strange shoes humans wore to protect their delicate feet.

My own furry paws were tender and swollen from my long journey. Perhaps humans had the right idea.

My ponderings were cut short when the human, another man, judging by his mild smell, paused in front of the shed that contained the carrot-scent I'd detected earlier.

He had a small patch of silver hair on his head, reminding me of Chesney's silvered fur. He pulled open the door and disappeared inside.

My brain raced as I considered whether to follow him. While it was unlikely that he'd see me, there was also the risk that I might be trapped inside. My foot thumped anxiously.

The human exited, carrying something I didn't

have a name for until he moved not far off and began thrusting the stick at the ground, removing large chunks of dirt. A shovel. Durrell was right—there was no end to the strange tricks these humans had come up with to overcome their inadequacies.[8]

The human paused to wipe a drip of sweat from his forehead. I was studying the appendages on his hand—his fingers—when I realized that the door to the shed was wide open.

The smell of carrots pulled me out from under the bush.

Ignoring the stiffness in my limbs and the soreness in my paws, I raced inside.

The place was nothing like my burrow at home. The walls were smooth and lined with shelves holding human contraptions of all shapes and sizes.

I sat up on my hind legs and sniffed. The carrot scent was strongest in the back. I hopped toward a shadowed corner, sniffing this and that along the way. The aroma of carrots grew stronger, but there was nothing along the floor that could be carrots, much

---

8. *On the off chance you are a human, I mean no disrespect. You can hardly help it that your hands aren't designed for digging.*

less seeds. The lowest shelves held what I thought were pots and a variety of other devices I couldn't make sense of. My nose twitched. The carrots had to be above my head.

Far above my head.

If only I were a transport rabbit, a jump like this would be no problem. But my scrawny legs were shaking. I gathered every bit of strength I had left, leaped, and fell flat on my rear. (Don't laugh—I was exhausted after a long night of hopping.)

I forced myself to rise.

This time I squatted, tensed my muscles, leaped— and made it.

There were no carrots on the shelf, but it overflowed with apple-sized seed bags. (Durrell brought an apple back to the Warren once. We were all enamored with the shiny red skin, but the fruit was too sour to be edible.) I smelled each burlap bag, my nose leading me ever closer to the precious purple carrot seeds.

Finally! I nudged a bag, releasing a smell so sweet, so welcome, that I nearly fell off the shelf. But three more bags had the same carrot scent. I turned my head slightly so as to better study them. (Remember the bit about our eyes being on the sides of our heads? It's great for making sure predators can't sneak up behind us, but not so great when we're trying to see what's right in front of our noses.)

I was about to sniff each one again when I realized the smell of carrots was also drifting toward me from the end of the shelf. I hopped over to investigate. Another bag of carrot seeds rested in a small container tucked behind several bags that smelled like chard. I carried the misplaced bag over to the others.

The markings on the bags were all unique, but the smells were the same. Durrell once talked about all the different carrots humans grew—orange carrots and sunny yellow carrots, in addition to the purple ones we ate.

I couldn't risk bringing back the wrong one—I'd have to take them all. I'd dropped the first four bags into my pouch and gripped the fifth in my mouth when the human returned. I froze, praying he wouldn't look my way.

We were invisible to the human eye at night, but a discerning eye could detect us by the light of day.

He rested the shovel in a corner and brushed

his hand through his hair before picking up what I thought must be a pail (a device apparently used to haul water).

A single twitch later, he exited. The door started to creak shut behind him.

With the bag of seeds still hanging from my mouth, I leaped from the shelf and dove for the exit.

BANG! The door slammed behind me, ruffling my fur.

I was free! And I'd gotten the seeds! I binkied in the bright sunlight.

I was so proud of my success, so busy imagining the heroic reception I'd receive back at the Warren, that I didn't notice the young girl who had flung herself under a nearby willow tree. A girl who paid careful attention to everything that happened in her garden. A girl who spotted the faintest shadow of a rabbit hopping from her shed. A girl who jumped up and yelled, "Hey! Those are mine!"

(That's right, my friends, I'd been discovered by Fleurine d'Aubigné.)

Chapter Three: *Fleurine*

The problem with stories is that you can never be absolutely certain that they're true. Take this one, for example. It'd be easy enough for me to convince you that the Angora Roux are perfect—maybe even heroic. After all, they were specially created by the Grande Maman in the Moon, and they brave all the dangers of the world to deliver Chou to any planter with a bundle of purple carrots in it every single night without fail.

But that version of the story wouldn't be entirely accurate. Because no matter what the rest of Montpeyroux might claim, even rabbits make mistakes. Especially the thieving skunk-rabbit that nearly ruined my life. In fact, at one point I would have gone so far as to call him a villain—a selfish, trouble-causing, carrot-gnawing, twitchy-eared villain.

Now I know better. He's no more a villain than I am.

But I'm getting ahead of myself. If you're to understand any of this, we're going to need to back up. Don't worry, I'm not going to tell you my whole life story— we can start with the morning the theft occurred—a morning that began the same as any other. Or maybe not *exactly* like any other. That morning, I was on a mission. I'd thrown on my plainest linen dress (still far fancier than I preferred) and slipped outside, surprised that the sweltering heat had already taken the normally refreshing morning air hostage.

Bright pink bougainvillea crept up the side of our home. A flower garden stretched out at the bottom of the terrace, its pebbled paths lined with clematis, gerberas, lilies, daffodils, and soft orange clusters of tempest's lace. Behind that was an enormous vegetable garden, supplying enough food for our cook, Bernadette, to get us through the summer—and there was plenty to store for winter, too.

My fingers tingled with longing as I passed the garden. I wanted to push back the cucumber leaves and search for the long green vegetables hidden underneath. To examine the tomatoes for the pests Jean-André had said plagued the plants the previous year. To spend all day in the garden, testing differences in soil, water, and seed depth—preparing to one day become a proper botanist.

Unfortunately, Maman once found me reading a volume of *Advances in Plant Knowledge*, which summarized all the current theories and latest breakthroughs. I was getting to the part about how some scientists believed plants moved pollen from one part of themselves to another in order to produce seeds when Maman snatched the book away from me.

She not only banned me from reading it, but she'd also gone so far as to forbid me from helping Jean-André garden. (Thankfully, she hadn't asked where the book came from. I would never lie to Maman, but I can't imagine the trouble it would have caused if she found out one of her conseillères encouraged my interest in science.)

She didn't understand that one day I hoped to unlock the secrets of Montpeyroux's elusive purple carrots—perhaps even the Chou de vie. To do that, I needed to study botany. Real botany, not sitting around sketching pretty flowers at the Day Lily Académie. I'd heard of académies of science opening up in other countries, but Maman wouldn't so much as consider the idea for fear of offending the Grand Maman in the Moon.

That's not to say I was entirely without hope. Jean-André insisted I follow Maman's orders and stay out of the garden he'd planted, but he looked the other way when he discovered that I'd taken over a small corner in the very back of the yard for my own uses.

I didn't dare take up enough space to draw Maman's attention, so I was confined to no more than one small crop at a time. I'd planted a batch of purple carrot seeds twenty-three days earlier, and while I knew they needed at least a month more to mature, I couldn't wait any longer to see if my crop was successful.

It was my third batch of purple carrots, but the first hadn't sprouted and the second had resulted in mostly stubby white carrots—only a few of them showed any signs of a purple tinge. (I'd tried leaving a bunch out for the rabbits anyway, but the carrots had still been there the next day, the planter otherwise empty.)

I'd had great success with other members of the

Apiaceae family—Bernadette had raved about my celery and turnips—prior to my purple carrot experiments, so I couldn't make sense of my failure. Since most purple carrots were grown on small farms that dotted the country, I suspected it had something to do with the soil at our city home, which was thicker and more clay-like than the rich, sandy soil at our cottage in the country. If only we'd ever spend enough time there for me to test my theory!

In the meantime, I'd watered this crop twice as often as the previous two, hoping that might help. I fetched a shiny bucket from the well-organized shed. Jean-André preferred I gather water from the rain barrels, but the reflection pond was closer. Goldfish darted through the placid pool, undoubtedly hoping I'd come to gift them fresh mealworms or crickets. The lip of the bucket broke the surface, sending ripples across the pond. Water rushed inside, nearly causing me to lose my grip. I heaved the full pail up. Its thin handle cut into my palm as I made my way back to my carrots.

After glancing at the house to make sure no one was watching, I sank to my knees and tipped the bucket over the parched soil, taking care to avoid the carrots' delicate greens so as not to scorch them in the already hot sun. The water disappeared almost immediately, sucked up by the thirsty ground. Working ever so gently, I nudged the thick, heavy dirt aside, my heart pounding so loudly in my ears that it drowned out the blue jays chirping in the trees.

Please let it be purple, please let it be purple, please let it be purple . . .

Purple carrot seeds were available at the market to anyone with enough coins to pay their ever-increasing prices—as long as they were over the age of eighteen. It had taken several weeks for me to find a vendor willing to break that law for a twelve-year-old and then another few days to convince him to sell to the Grande Lumière's daughter. (He said Maman would have his head if she ended up with another child because of my meddling, but that was ridiculous; no one in Montpeyroux had ever been beheaded, and Maman certainly wasn't about to start the practice now. Still, it took an extra handful of coins to convince him that I'd never rat him out in the first place.)

Here I must confess: my interest in this particular

crop was something more than the detached interest of a scientist. I'd tried for years to convince Maman that we needed another child in the house, but she always insisted that the line of succession was secure with me. Besides, she said she was far too busy running the country to fuss with another child. *Too busy.* That was precisely why I needed a sibling. (A little sister, preferably.)

The spotlight would be ever so much more bearable if I didn't have to stand in it alone, if I had someone to confide in. I knew I'd fall in love with my little sister the moment her face first peeked out from the Chou de vie. Maman would fall in love, too. Her face lit up when she held other people's babies, tenderly tickling them under the chin as she cooed soft greetings. With this crop of purple carrots, my dream would finally come true.

I brushed the last bit of soil aside, revealing the top of a carrot. A white, misshapen carrot.

My hands dropped to my lap. My eyes stung as I blinked back tears.

I'd bought purple seeds. Paid triple the already steep price. The vendor had insisted that there were no guarantees—not even purple carrot seeds could *guarantee* purple carrots. (In case you're confused: legend has it that the shiny purple seeds used to produce nothing but purple carrots, but over time that changed. No one knows why, but mark my words, one day I'll figure it out.)

I'd been so sure I'd get purple carrots in this crop— my *heart* had been so sure.

This is only one carrot, I reminded myself. Mud coated my fingers as I scooped away the soil from the carrot next to it.

White. Along with the carrot next to it and the carrot after that. I dug frantically, sure that somewhere in the crop, I'd find a handful of purple carrots. (Rabbits required five for a delivery, which seemed like a waste. Unless they had vastly different taste buds, the carrots were all but inedible. One of Maman's wealthy supporters once served purple carrots at a dinner party— even covered in a heavy gravy, they were sickeningly sweet—nothing like the delicious orange carrots Jean-André grew.)

Fat earthworms wiggled and squirmed, angry that I'd disturbed them.

With each white carrot, a little hope drained from my chest. There were only a dozen carrots left when I scooped aside a handful of dirt and spotted a bit of purple. I frantically brushed more dirt aside, then sat back and let out a puff of frustrated air. This one was tinged purple on top but white otherwise. I'd let my last batch grow to maturity, hoping the white was a stage in their life cycle, but now I knew these white carrots would never turn purple.

"Fleurine!"

My maid's voice tore through the garden.

The fiery sun glowered at me from high in the sky. Uh-oh.

I jumped to my feet and rubbed my hands together, groaning at the dirt caked under my nails. If Maman caught sight of me, I'd be deep in a rotten pile of cabbage.

"Fleurine!" Elodie called again.

"Coming!" With a last, longing glance at the remaining carrots, I hurried toward the house.

As I neared the stairs, Elodie's hands fell to her hips. Her hazel eyes flashed with disapproval. "Your Maman is going to be hopping mad if she finds out you've been digging in the dirt again."

"I know," I said, brushing past her.

Maman was no doubt tied up with her own preparations for the ceremony to come, but I breathed a sigh of relief when I reached my quarters without detection. The housemaids had already come and gone. The gauzy lilac curtains I pulled around my bedframe at night to make the otherwise vast space feel cozier were tied back, and my blankets were smooth.

I hurried to a bowl on my washstand and scrubbed the dirt from my hands. The clear water turned a mucky brown color. Elodie frowned. "You couldn't have held off for one day?"

I'd meant to—I'd promised myself that I wouldn't spend any time in the garden this morning. But then I woke up early, and I couldn't get back to sleep, and it was such a big day for Maman that I guess part of me thought maybe it would be a big day for me, too.

Maybe it still would be. The minute the ceremony—and Maman's luncheon—was over, I planned to finish checking the carrots. Elodie handed me a kerchief to dry my hands and then helped me out of my dirt-streaked dress and into the new one Maman had specially ordered for today's ceremony. The stiff iris-colored satin was lined with lace at the bottom, lace around the short sleeves—even lace around my neck.

I couldn't help but scratch my throat as I settled on a cushioned stool in front of a mahogany dressing table. Floor-to-ceiling windows filled the room with light and showcased the gardens below.

"Stop scratching," Elodie said. "Do you really want to explain a rash to your maman?"

I dropped my hand, and she started brushing out my glossy, chestnut-colored hair with long, even strokes.

Outside, a monarch butterfly flitted and twirled, its yellow and black wings vivid against the bright blue sky.

Elodie hit a knot.

"Ouch!" I yelped.

"Apologies, my lady." The reflection in the window allowed me to see Elodie push a summer squash-colored curl from her face. If I turned around, the first thing I'd notice was the single freckle perched on the tip of her pert nose.

"A kiss from the rabbits," she once told me,

claiming that freckles were a sign of good luck. She was right, too—large families weren't common in Montpeyroux, but she was the oldest of five. Not five siblings—five sisters.

I'd studied my lightly tanned face in the mirror for hours after that, willing even the smallest of freckles to appear. Once, I'd even stolen Maman's charcoal pencil and dotted my skin. Maman had initially accused her maid of theft. When she saw what I'd done, she'd lectured me for ages (and forced me to apologize to the poor maid, which I thought was unfair since I wasn't the one who had accused her).

Elodie worked more gently as she combed and tugged my hair into an elegant knot and then fastened a lace cap over the top.

"There," she said. "Don't you look the pretty picture."

I swirled around and glanced carelessly at the mirror she held up. The girl that shined back at me appeared every bit the Grande Lumière's perfect daughter, an attractive girl with intelligent eyes and flawless skin, a girl of good breeding and impeccable manners, a girl being groomed to one day step into her maman's shoes. (The d'Aubigné family had always governed Montpeyroux, and Maman was determined the tradition wouldn't stop with her.)

But I didn't care one carrot about looking the pretty picture or one day stepping into Maman's shoes. I hated these affairs, the endless public appearances and stuffy luncheons Maman made me attend. Today was going to be worse than most—it was the ribbon-cutting for Maman's pet project.

The building was sure to be magnificent, and the opening of the first national theater in the entire country was expected to boast record attendance. The city was already crowded as people flocked to attend the Summer Festival. There would be hundreds—thousands—of eyes all focused on Maman, on me standing at her side.

"Can't you come with me?" I asked.

"Your maman gave me the afternoon off," Elodie chirped.

Her obvious happiness stung. She would have free time while I was forced to attend one social obligation after another, shuffled about like a fancy soufflé on display for all the country to see. (Though Maman didn't usually travel during the Summer Festival, rumors of unrest from the Northern Corridor couldn't be ignored. She was leaving right after the ceremony and subsequent luncheon—I'd originally hoped this meant all of our obligations would be canceled for the next few days, and I could either spend my time in the garden or escape to our cottage, but she'd insisted that I was old enough to appear in her stead.)

"I suppose you'll be meeting up with your sisters?" I asked Elodie.

"I mean to, my lady. We're going to watch the ceremony and then picnic in the Gardens."

The Gardens would be crowded with people; vendors would be selling everything from carrot pudding to rabbit carvings to dolls wrapped in velvety Chou-like leaves. Children would run and play, and the air would be rich with laughter.

"I wish I could join you." The words slipped out before I could think better of them. Maman would never allow such a thing, but it was the truth—I was envious of Elodie's four sisters, of the happiness that sparked in her eyes whenever she spoke of them. Of the fun they'd have together.

She'd been with us a little over a year—ever since Maman decided I was old enough to let the nurse-maid go—and in the beginning I hoped we'd be fast friends. But except for the rare occasions when I pried out stories of her sisters' shenanigans, she engaged only to answer my questions and perform her duties. It's not that she wasn't nice, but there was a wall between us that I couldn't figure out how to knock down.

Her mouth twitched as though she might have something to say. Instead, she fussed with the pin on my hat.

"Perfect!" she said.

I wrinkled my nose and turned back to the window.

The butterfly bumped and fluttered against the glass. Poor thing. It wouldn't try so hard to get in if it knew how I longed to escape.

The front bell rang, signaling it was time for our departure. Elodie curtseyed and scurried from the room, her cheeks flushed with excitement.

I gave myself a once-over and noticed a broken nail. *Rotten carrots!* Maman letting that slide was more than I could hope for. I dabbed a bit of lavender perfume—a soft, earthy scent that reminded me of the countryside—on my wrists and pulled on a pair of white gloves that hadn't been planned as part of my ensemble.

Maman wouldn't be pleased with the last-minute addition—she preferred that our thick gold rings, featuring the rose from our family coat of arms, be on display during public events. *Don't underestimate the importance of symbols*, she always said. *They bear great power.*

I would be glad to spend even a single day without the heavy ring on my hand, but Maman's hawkish eyes would notice its absence when I removed the gloves to dine, and a recent growth spurt made wearing the tightly fitted ring on top of the fabric impossible.

I rushed down the grand central staircase, avoiding the disapproving gazes of the generations of d'Aubignés hanging on the wall. I was tempted to stop and sniff the gorgeous bouquet of flowers that graced the table at the bottom, but I didn't dare. At the front door, I steeled myself and then stepped into the hot, swampy air. It'd be a miracle if I got through the day without wilting.

My gaze slid to the empty planter built into the front

of our house. The soil inside the glass enclosure was barren now, but I'd give anything to leave a bundle of purple carrots and find a Chou de vie planted in their stead. *It could happen*, I reminded myself, thinking of the still-buried carrots at the back of the house.

Maman and two of her conseillères stood outside the gold-plated carriage. A purple flag embroidered with our coat of arms hung from a pole jutting up from the roof. Upon seeing me, Madame Pauline's lips turned up slightly. She was tall and angular, with black skin and a head full of short, tight curls. Her demeanor was normally stern, but she and I shared a secret affinity for science. Madame Blanchet was petite, with pale skin and silver hair cut in severe lines around a long, narrow face. She was never unkind, but I didn't care for the way her icy gray eyes brushed over me dismissively.

Maman looked every bit as resplendent as one might expect. Her voluptuous figure was shown off by a ruby-colored dress that contrasted with her lily-white skin and gleaming black tresses, practically ensuring every eye would be glued to her during the ceremony. An elegant hat completed her ensemble.

Why must we always be perfect? I'd once asked her.

The country doesn't want a normal person leading them, Maman had said. *They want someone they can aspire to, someone who represents the best of what Montpeyroux has to offer.*

I adjusted my cap. "Good day, Maman."

I longed for her to gather me in her arms and call me her petite Chou, but she hadn't done that since I moved out of the nursery. Her sharp eyes scanned me from head to foot, searching for the slightest of flaws. Her gaze lingered on my gloves. She arched an eyebrow, a subtle message that left no doubt she was on to me. "Come along," she said, leaving a trail of jasmine-scented air behind her as she climbed into the carriage. "We mustn't be late."

I settled next to her on the stiff seat. Like the rest of the interior, it was covered in thick red velvet. I longed to run my hand over it, to change the color from dark to light, but Maman always said fidgeting was for children, not for proper young ladies. Mesdames Pauline and Blanchet arranged themselves across from us.

As the carriage lurched into motion, Maman and her conseillères reviewed protocol for the ribbon-cutting ceremony. When they mentioned opening with the annual Blessing of the Carrots, I jumped in. "Couldn't we keep the bundle for ourselves this year?"

"Fleurine," Maman said sharply, "Do not interrupt. And you know that's impossible. A family has already been selected."

My gaze dropped to the carriage floor as I waited for the lecture on how she was far too busy to take on the responsibility of another child and how our family was perfect exactly as it was. Perfect, except I was a single sapling growing in a lonely meadow.

Instead, Maman and the conseillères returned to reviewing the ceremony, then moved on to Maman's trip, breaking only long enough for her to remind me to mind my posture.

(I don't mean to make Maman out to be a monster. She's firm in her belief that too much softness will render me unable to bear the responsibilities I'll one day have to shoulder.)

With my spine straight and my chin up, I watched the city roll by. I did my best to avoid looking at the planters outside every residence, but the entire city teemed with evidence of children. A young maman bent over a pram making silly faces at the baby inside. Three young boys played Fetch the Carrot with a flop-eared puppy. The smiling faces of two girls with matching braids shined from a second-floor window.

Although the streets swelled with people flocking to attend the ceremony, the crowds parted for our carriage. I was lost in my observations when sharp voices caught my attention.

Maman's conseillères had taken to arguing more and more often lately, nearly always about the rising costs of necessities such as food and purple carrots. A series of recent droughts had forced people to give up their farms and move to the city in search of steady incomes.

"The people are growing frustrated. They're demanding help," Madame Pauline said. "We need to look to science. Innovation."

"Nonsense," Madame Blanchet said. "The Grande Maman in the Moon will provide for us—she always does."

"The Grande Maman in the Moon can't help us if

we don't help ourselves," Madame Pauline shot back. "We can't sit back as food production continues to drop and prices continue to rise. People can't afford to eat, much less buy purple carrots."

"What do you expect us to do about that?" Madame Blanchet said. "We can't force people to farm. And we can't force the crops we already have to grow any more quickly—if the Grande Maman in the Moon wanted them to grow faster, they would."

"I'm not sure you're right," Madame Pauline said. "Research is being done in other countries—there may be more to farming than Grande Maman calling to the plants."

Madame Blanchet waved her arm dismissively. "What a load of rabbit droppings. You'd better pray the Grande Maman doesn't hear you talking such nonsense. You can hardly afford another illness."

"That's quite enough," Maman said. "Madame Blanchet is right. If the Grande Maman in the Moon wanted us to intervene, she would let us know. In the meantime, we've already increased basket distributions to help the hungry."

"Increasing aid is important, but it's not a long-term

solution," Madame Pauline said, addressing Maman in a respectful tone.

"Things are out of balance now, but nature always rights itself," Maman said.

She sounded certain, but I wasn't so sure. The Grande Maman in the Moon had honored our family with the responsibility of running the country—we even had a small chunk of moon rock on display at home to prove it. But that was back at the beginning of time. To my knowledge, none of us had heard from her since.

I couldn't believe she'd really punish us for doing everything we could—including using science—to help her people. (For all we knew, maybe the drought was punishment for *not* using science.) Then again, the last time Madame Pauline had tried to convince Maman to allow scientists into the country, she'd taken ill with a fever for more than a week.

Judging by the way the muscles in Madame Pauline's jaw bulged, she shared my frustration. But she remained silent as Maman began discussing the broken cobblestones on Rougine Boulevard.

We inched our way forward, eventually pulling up

in front of a massive building designed to impress and delight. A wide set of stairs led to a terrace guarded on either side by two stone rabbits, each nearly the size of our carriage. The double front doors were carved with rabbits, carrots, and Chou de vie. Even the leaded windows were etched with the outlines of rabbits.

A footman opened the door. The smell of sugared almonds from a nearby vendor filled our carriage. Maman sucked in a deep breath and then, as though taken over by a puppet master, squared her shoulders and exited, smiling as though she hadn't a care in the world.

I followed, uncomfortably aware of the hundreds of eyes turned our way. If only I could melt into the crowd. Or join the group of children climbing the long limbs of a nearby apple tree.

Maman's most prominent supporters waited on the terrace. She took the time to shake every hand, to ask some personal detail about each of their lives. *Leadership is about thinking big but paying attention to the details,* she always said. *There's no better way to cultivate loyalty than to show you care.*

I smiled and shook each hand behind Maman,

pretending there was nowhere I'd rather be. I had acquaintances at school, of course, but none of them shared my interest in gardening or botany. (I learned this lesson the hard way when I invited a classmate home after school to search for worms. She'd screeched and told everyone in class I was a worm-lover. After that, no one wanted to pair with me during dance lessons, claiming that my hands were full of worm germs.)

Even if I wanted to pursue a friendship, my schedule left little room for such things. Maman and I were required to attend a never-ending stream of parties and events put on by her wealthy supporters. (I occasionally tried to beg out of them, but Maman claimed they were a small price to pay for the privileged lives we led. Easy for her to say—she delighted in all the attention.)

There was never time for slowing down, for getting to know kids my own age beyond sharing polite conversations in stuffy ballrooms. Other than Madame Pauline, I'd never met anyone who shared my interests or cared about *me* rather than my social status.

Finally, Maman's supporters took their seats, and

she stepped up to the podium that had been erected at the top of the stairs. While the crowd below dabbed at the sweat dripping down their necks, Maman appeared every bit as fresh as a spring breeze. I shifted uncomfortably in my chair, wishing I could fan my skirt. A despondent-looking child in the front row sucked her thumb and clung to her maman's leg. If she were my sister, she'd be required to sit quietly next to me, but we'd squeeze each other's hands, sending silent sister signals that we weren't alone.

"Ladies and gentlemen, friends and neighbors," Maman said. "Thank you for gathering with us this morning to celebrate what is sure to be one of the proudest moments of my seventeen-year tenure."

Maman took over at a young age after her own mother passed away unexpectedly. Despite the recent unrest, she was one of the most popular Grande Lumières in our country's history.

"A true leader is measured by the happiness of her people, and I have every faith that this new endeavor will enrich the lives of everyone in our fine city."

What about my happiness—why didn't she ever worry about that?

"Before we celebrate this monumental event, it's my privilege and honor to mark the opening of the Summer Festival with the Blessing of the Carrots."

Madame Pauline passed Maman a bundle of purple carrots tied in fancy lavender ribbons.

Was it my imagination or did Maman's glance flicker in my direction? For the briefest of moments, I allowed myself a glimmer of hope. Then Maman invited a young couple to join her on stage. Joy shined from their smiling faces. Judging from their fine clothing, they could have purchased their own purple carrots. *What a shame.*

With the steep increase in carrot prices over the recent months, I thought the general lottery should've been dropped in favor of a family that was unable to afford a bunch of carrots on their own. Maman disagreed, claiming the Grande Maman in the Moon had given us our traditions for a reason. In any case, being the recipient of the bundle blessed by Maman was a tremendous honor—the child was sure to live a life of good fortune.

I fought the urge to snatch the bundle from Maman's hands and take off running.

She held the carrots reverently as she addressed the crowd. "Please join me in thanking the Grande Maman in the Moon for blessing us with the gift of life. Through her grace, the Angora Roux . . ."

A child in the front row clutched a familiar book to her chest. *The Legends of Grand-Maman Rabbit.* Every child in Montpeyroux was raised with tales of mythical rabbits called the Angora Rex. The stories were filled with the giant rabbits' heroics—how they jumped high enough to hang candles in the sky for us to see at night, how they landed carefully to create the craters for our lakes and seas, how they stretched tiny shrubs until they became the towering trees we have today. According to the stories, the Rex were wiped out when a carrot plague destroyed the enormous carrots they needed to survive.

I asked Maman once if there might be any truth to the tales, but she'd hushed me, insisting that such wonderings dishonored the Grande Maman in the Moon, that it wasn't our place to question her designs but rather to appreciate her blessings and work to deserve them.

I didn't see how wanting to understand how our

world worked dishonored the Grande Maman, but I knew better than to argue and risk subjecting myself to Maman's disappointment.

The crowd cheered as Maman finished the Blessing and handed the bundle to the happy father-to-be, who raised it jubilantly in the air. I scanned the crowd, searching for Elodie.

My lips stretched into a smile when I spotted her, but she giggled with her sisters, not paying one carrot of attention to Maman and certainly not meeting my gaze. My shoulders drooped as I swatted away a pesky fly.

Maman talked a bit more about the theater, then picked up an enormous set of shears to clip the yellow ribbon stretched across the front door. Shouting came from the back of the crowd.

"We don't need a theater, we need food!" a thin young man with neatly parted hair yelled. Two others appeared beside him, a man and a lady, both about his age and both shouting about their empty stomachs.

Maman's lips tightened. She nodded to a set of guards stationed discreetly at the edge of the crowd. They removed the protestors, who continued yelling grievances even as they were dragged away.

As their shouts faded, uncomfortable titters arose from the shocked crowd. I trembled. I'd heard of protests in other countries, but such things never happened in Montpeyroux. Maman calmly apologized for the interruption, reassured everyone that the Grande Maman in the Moon had heard their concerns, and reminded them of the esteem the entire country would garner as the first on the continent to boast a national theater.

Her poise left no doubt that she had everything under control. The crowd relaxed. It took me longer to settle, but I forced myself to focus on the snip of Maman's scissors cutting through the ribbon. On the roar of excitement that filled the air.

The crowd swept forward, jostling to enter. Once the rush thinned to a trickle, I slipped inside. I'd been dragged to the construction site with Maman numerous times over the last several months, but those visits hadn't prepared me for the finished building, for the sunlight streaming in through the glass dome overhead, for the way it bounced off the sparkling chandeliers. For the murmur of voices echoing across the marble floors.

The wonder of it, the way the patrons rushed from one area to the next, gasping and giggling with their friends and family, their faces alight with awe, made me feel lonelier than ever. I wandered the lobby, wishing I were back home in the garden.

"Fleurine!"

I spun around. Elodie's glowing face greeted me. Her sisters crowded around her. "Isn't it a wonder? They're performing *The Legends of Grand-Maman Rabbit* this evening, and children are invited to attend for free!"

Her enthusiasm was contagious. "It is delightful, isn't it?"

The youngest of Elodie's sisters, a girl of no more than five years, spoke up. "I've never been to a theater!"

"Pardon her interruption, Miss. This is my youngest sister, Camilla."

Elodie introduced the rest of her sisters, who blushed and curtseyed. Though their dresses were several seasons out of fashion, they were obviously freshly washed and ironed. The colorful fabrics, combined with the different colors of the girls' eyes, hair, and skin, made them prettier than a spring bouquet.

"It's lovely to meet you all," I said, smiling warmly and barely restraining myself from pinching Camilla's adorably chubby cheeks. "*Grand-Maman Rabbit* was one of my favorite bedtime stories growing up. I'm certain you'll enjoy the play."

"It's my favorite story, too!" Camilla's amber eyes sparkled with wonder.

Another of Elodie's sisters tugged at her arm. "Come on! We're going to miss the egg hunt."

Elodie laughed. "Please excuse us, Miss. The egg hunt awaits us."

The sisters executed another series of uncoordinated curtseys and then tumbled away, a giggling whirl of ribbons. If their family had its own classification, it would be *Homindae perfectus*.

I blinked back hot tears and made my way to the dark theater, where I tucked into a seat in the corner. I was happy for Elodie, truly. But that happiness only made my own longing all the more unbearable.

Chapter Four: *Fleurine*

Maman and her conseillères were flushed with success when they climbed into the carriage.

"People traveled from around the whole country to attend the opening," Madame Blanchet said, flipping open a delicate fan hand-painted with white carrot blooms.

"My patrons seemed happy," Maman said. "I expect they'll be eager to open their purses at the luncheon. Speaking of the luncheon—" She turned to me. "I have a surprise for you."

I couldn't help bouncing a little on my seat. "What is it?"

"I plan to share the news after we eat," she said. "But I think you'll be quite pleased."

Her demeanor shifted as she addressed Madame Blanchet. "Speaking of surprises. You assured me there wouldn't be any security breaches today."

Security breaches—did she mean the protestors? I wondered what had happened to them after they were taken away. The matter would undoubtedly be handled by one of Maman's appointees.

While Madame Blanchet defended her preparations, I pressed my hands under my legs to keep from fidgeting. My mind spun faster than the carriage's wheels as I pondered Maman's surprise. Maybe she'd planned an addition to our garden? Jean-André had been pressing her for a greenhouse. Or . . . could it be?

I was so excited by the thought that floated through my head that I could hardly finish it. What if Maman had finally realized how much a sibling meant to me? I wiggled my toes, a trick I'd learned to get rid of excess energy while keeping the rest of my body still.

The carriage pulled up behind several others in front of the home of the Mesdames Archambeau, two of Maman's most ardent supporters. The house was nearly as grand as our own, boasting several floors and a formal entry lined with staff waiting to meet our every need.

The mesdames greeted us in a large marble hall. The first Madame Archambeau had warm brown skin and shiny black hair that towered high overhead, while her wife's fat silver curls framed a powdered white face rendered almost comical by too much rouge. Their daughter, Abeline Archambeau, stood primly at their side in a ghastly sage-colored dress that did little to complement her sallow complexion.

I groaned. Abeline was one year ahead of me in school and every bit as stuffy and pretentious as her parents. Perhaps after exchanging pleasantries, I could claim I was indisposed and sneak away to the quiet of their library. But no, there was Maman's announcement to wait for.

The next hour was insufferably dull. I perched at the edge of a brocade settee in the crowded salon, making small talk with the silver-haired Madame Archambeau, mostly listening to her boast about Abeline's various accomplishments in art and music, as the room grew ever hotter.

"Please, excuse me," I finally said, leaping from the

settee. A footman gave me directions to the washroom, but along the way, I passed a set of glass doors leading to a lush thinking garden. Without thinking at all, I pushed through the doors.

The outdoor air was even warmer than inside, but the hot breeze was a welcome relief. I wandered the pebbled path circling the reflecting pond and paused to admire the thick, healthy leaves on a flowering plant I didn't recognize. The orange petals reminded me of a daylily, but instead of opening upward, the blooms faced downward and were covered in dark spots. I suspected it was part of the Asphodelaceae family, but I made a mental note to look it up in the book I kept hidden at the bottom of my wardrobe.

After stroking the soft petals, I meant to make my way back inside, but a small frog perched on a lily pad caught my attention with a deep croak.

"Hello, little fellow," I said, squatting on the pond's edge. I expected the frog to hop away, but when I pulled off my gloves and reached out a hand, he allowed me to scoop him up. His wet feet were cool against my sweaty palm.

"What are you doing out here?" I asked. "Is this your home?"

I scanned the area, checking to see if the frog had any family waiting for his return.

The door creaked open, startling me.

"Miss?" a spindly footman said.

I set the frog in a small patch of soil under one of the blooming daylily-like flowers and jumped up. "Yes?"

"The party is retiring to the dining room. Perhaps you'd like to join them?"

Heat blossomed in my cheeks. Maman must have sent him after me. I tucked a stray hair behind my ear, pulled on my gloves, and hurried inside. The dining room was a gaudy space that boasted several nude statues along with an array of colorful parrots in gilded cages.

Most of the nearly three dozen guests had already been seated, overwhelming the room with their heavy floral perfumes. I took my place with Maman on one side and Abeline on the other.

"Where were you?" Maman hissed under her breath.

"I—"

"What is that on your cheek?"

I swiped at my face. A smear of dirt appeared on my white glove. I must have gotten my hand dirty when I set the frog down and then touched my face.

I was saved from Maman's lecture by Abeline, who asked if I was enjoying the party.

"I met the most delightful frog in your thinking garden," I said.

Her face twisted and I realized that, in her mind, the words *delightful* and *frog* didn't belong in the same sentence.

"You touched a frog?"

"A little one."

She tried to hide her disgust behind a polite smile. "I only go out there to sketch. It's the perfect spot to practice water, don't you think?"

I could never find the patience to sit and try to recreate something on paper for hours on end (or even minutes, truth be told), but I was saved from answering by Abeline prattling on about a sketch her maman wanted to frame and how she planned to work on faces next, but she didn't know if she'd ever be able to capture anyone's eyes properly because—

When will Maman make her announcement? I thought, rubbing my forehead.

"Are you unwell?" Abeline asked.

I was tempted to take the opportunity to excuse myself again, but instead I begged forgiveness. "I'm only tired from the excitement of the day."

I removed my gloves and tried to hide my broken nail as I picked at my plate, which was laden with chocolate-covered strawberries and dainty rabbit-shaped sandwiches. My gaze rested on the window across the room. In the distance, a thin wisp of gray smoke spiraled into the air from Mignon's crematorium.

I'd never seen the place. Although I'd asked Maman if we could take a tour, she said our job was to inspire and encourage, not to call attention to anything that might cause distress. I suspected her reluctance also had something to do with the crematorium's location in the "less desirable" part of town (and her fear of catching head lice, which apparently ran rampant among the masses).

Still, I was curious about the process. I'd read that

the ashes were swept into a hole after they cooled, and that Angora Roux came every night to pick out the soul seeds. Most people believed they used the seeds to grow new Chou de vie, though no one had ever been able to prove it. (Possessing soul seeds is illegal now, but apparently people used to try to grow Chou all the time and never got so much as a sprout.)

If only Maman would open an académie of science. Surely a few seeds could be approved for that. If not, we could still study purple carrots. Once we understood what caused them to make seeds and why they grew, we could find a way to produce more of them. With an increase in supply, the price would drop.

Maman finally rose from her chair. She tapped a spoon on a crystal glass etched with carrots. After the room quieted, she cleared her throat and launched into a speech thanking her supporters for making her long-held vision of Montpeyroux's first national theater a reality.

I tapped my foot impatiently.

"And now," Maman finally said, shining a dazzling smile at her captive audience, "I'm thrilled to announce my next project."

"Never one to rest, are you?" someone called out.

"Ever a devoted public servant," Maman answered. "But this project is perhaps even more near and dear to my heart than the theater, for it will firmly establish the next generation of leaders in Montpeyroux."

Holy cottontail! She said, "Leaders." With an "s." I had to be one of the leaders Maman was talking about. The plural made hope swell in my chest. Finally, a sibling!

"I've convinced the Mesdames Archambeau to open a new académie here in Mignon."

So no sibling, then. Still, my hope puffed up bigger than an Angora Rex. Maybe I'd gotten through to Maman about an académie of science, after all!

"Now, I know what you're asking yourselves." She paused for dramatic effect.

"You're asking why Mignon needs a new académie. The answer is simple. Times are changing. The country is changing. More than ever before, the leadership in Montpeyroux has to govern with a steady hand, to act as a shining beacon of hope."

Maman paused again. *Silence can be more powerful than words,* she always said.

"I am therefore delighted to announce that my new académie will focus on public rhetoric and personal discipline. In particular, there will be an emphasis on developing a thorough understanding of the traditions handed down by the Grande Maman in the Moon. Graduates will include Grande Lumières and their future conseillères."

I twisted my ring, which suddenly felt far too tight for my finger. Madame Blanchet sat across from Maman with a satisfied smile that bordered on gloating. Beside her, Madame Pauline's smile appeared strained.

Maman beamed at the crowd, which offered an enthusiastic round of applause. After it died down, she continued. "This académie will be extremely limited in size, with only a small class drawn each year from the very best and brightest around the country. It's my absolute delight to announce the first two students to lead the new class."

She turned her smile to me. I wished I could burrow down into the earth like one of the worms I loved finding in the garden.

"Fleurine and Abeline, congratulations and welcome to Montpeyroux's Académie of Leadership."

Just like that, Maman had sealed my fate. The room must have filled with applause, but I didn't hear it. Somehow my heart had jumped up to my head and was beating in my ears, blocking out all the sounds around me. My vision narrowed, blurring everything except Maman's smiling face.

Her full lips. Her shining white teeth. How come I never noticed before how big her two front teeth were? Like she was part rabbit.

I stared, unblinking, as Maman's mouth continued moving, continued opening and closing. Finally, Abeline nudged me.

"What? Pardon?" My vision opened up and my hearing returned with a deafening roar.

"Your maman wants us to say something," she whispered.

"Oh, yes, right," I said. "You go ahead."

Abeline stood up, adjusted the bow on her dress, and gave an eloquent speech about how proud she was to have been selected for this honor, how she'd work hard to make the city, and her country, proud. How together, we'd lift each other up and make life better for everyone.

It wasn't at all clear why she needed to attend the académie, polished as she was. I was an altogether different matter. I didn't care for attention at any point, and especially not when I hadn't been expecting it. Furthermore, how could I possibly be expected to sound cheerful about attending a school focused on leadership and traditions when all I wanted was to study botany?

Sympathy shined from Madame Pauline's eyes, which somehow made me feel worse.

I resisted the urge to tug at the lace trimming my neck. When Abeline sat down, I took my time standing up, hoping to stall until my brain pieced together something coherent—something that would make Maman look good.

She wanted me to speak, but she didn't want to hear what I really had to say.

"Um, thank you," I said.

Maman flashed a smile that everyone else would read as encouraging, but I could see the worry under it. *Don't let me down,* it said.

I drew in a deep breath as Maman had taught me to do. I was Fleurine d'Aubigné, daughter of the Grande Lumière. Delivering a speech worthy of anything less was unacceptable.

Someone in the crowd shifted.

Someone else coughed.

Maman's gaze hardened. *Get on with it.*

I couldn't tell the crowd how excited I was, but I had to say something. *When in doubt, focus on praise,* Maman always said.

"The Académie of Leadership is a wonderful idea. It will be a tremendous asset to Montpeyroux in the coming years."

I stopped, wondering what to say next. My thoughts tangled like the roots of several plants searching for water. Maman nodded for me to go on. Maman.

"My maman is a true visionary, always focused on improving the lives of Montpeyroux's citizens, always putting their needs before her own. I hope you'll add your support to her newest endeavor."

I sat down abruptly.

The diners offered lukewarm applause. Maman gave me a clipped nod. I hadn't dazzled her, but hopefully I'd done well enough to avoid a lecture later. My chest felt empty, as if Maman had ripped out my heart and buried it along with my dreams.

She leaned over and whispered in my ear, "Smile, darling. Someday, the entire country will be yours."

But I didn't want to smile. I wondered: Could you gift a country to someone who didn't want it?

The rest of the luncheon passed in a blur. Beside me, Abeline babbled incessantly about her excitement. About our futures. I smiled and played the part of the dutiful daughter. But I felt as though a vine had wrapped itself around my chest, threatening to strangle the air from my lungs.

The moment we climbed in the carriage, my emotions overflowed. "How could you?" I cried, clenching the edges of my seat.

Maman glanced at Madame Blanchet before asking, "Whatever are you talking about?"

I didn't care that her conseillères were here. That they'd hear everything. That I was embarrassing Maman. "You decided my whole life for me!"

"Is this about the académie?"

Of course it was about the académie. "I won't go."

"It's not up for discussion," Maman said coolly.

I folded my arms, not caring one carrot that I was

acting the part of a spoiled child. "You can't make me."

Maman rubbed her temples. "You hate Day Lily. You're constantly begging me to take you out."

"Yes! Because I want to attend an académie of *science*."

"You know that's out of the question. Besides, you're to be the next—"

But I was tired of being lectured about my duties. About my future. "Why can't you—"

Maman drew herself up tall. "Fleurine, that's quite enough. My conseillères and I have important business to discuss."

Her brisk voice made it clear that I'd crossed a line. Any more, and she'd threaten me with a nursemaid. But if she wanted me to act like a grown-up, then she should treat me like a grown-up and not run around making decisions behind my back.

My eyes burned. I pressed my lips together and willed myself to remain quiet as they reviewed the final details for Maman's trip.

Several minutes later, I exited the carriage, dutifully kissed Maman's cheek, and raced around the back of the house. I didn't mind my dress as I fell to my knees, yanked off my gloves, and swiped the now-dry dirt from around a feathery green carrot top.

I wanted a sibling. *Needed* a sibling—someone to talk to, someone who truly understood my frustrations, the constant pressure I was under to be the perfect daughter Maman expected. *Please let this carrot be purple. Please.*

A white carrot glared up at me.

My chest heaved as I moved on to the next carrot.

White.

This couldn't be happening.

I continued turning up white (or, at best, slightly tinged) carrot after carrot until only one remained. The hot sun soaked through my dress, threatening to crisp my back. I took a deep breath.

Please, Grande Maman in the Moon, I prayed. *Make this a purple carrot, and I'll never ask for another thing ever again.*

I lowered my fingers to the soil and dug.

The last carrot was white.

There would be no sibling for me. Not now, maybe never. I flopped down on my back and clenched a soft fistful of grass.

"Ouch!" I yelped, opening my palm. A bumblebee flew from my hand and buzzed angrily around my head.

I sat up. My palm swelled as hot tears flowed over my cheeks. Jean-André's lush vines filled with fat cucumbers seemed to mock me.

The door to the shed creaked, drawing my attention. Jean-André emerged, carrying a pail. Something dove out after him, narrowly escaping the shutting door. The creature looked like a rabbit, but it was faint and blurry, as if I were viewing it at a far-off distance through thick glass.

I jumped to my feet. Angora Roux were cloaked in some kind of magic that rendered them completely invisible at night—legend had it that they could be spotted during the day if one paid close enough attention, but since they only delivered when it was dark, no one really knew whether or not this was true. Until now.

This was definitely a Roux, but it didn't exactly look like the pictures and statues all over the city. The size of a small fox, nothing about it screamed cute and snuggly—not its painfully thin frame, not its tall, twitchy ears, and definitely not its skunk-like coloring. We didn't have skunks in Montpeyroux, but one of Maman's patrons had brought one in from somewhere overseas, removed its scent-pouch, and kept it as a pet. It looked like this rabbit—all black except for a thick white stripe running from its nose to its rump.

The Roux executed a strange leap, twisting its body in the air.

A pouch of seeds dangled from the rabbit's mouth. *My purple carrot seeds!*

"Hey!" I yelled. "Those are mine!"

The skunk-rabbit froze, then dropped the bag of seeds into its pouch and sprang into action, hopping toward the front gate.

The dirty rotten thief! I raced after it.

"Did you see that?" I yelled, dashing past our guard.

"See what?"

I followed the rabbit, dodging people and carriages.

For a moment, I thought I'd lost it, but then I spotted the rabbit's black fur as it crossed the street and turned into the Gardens. It hopped through the crowded pavilion smelling of toasted almonds, along a gravel path bustling with people out celebrating the start of the Summer Festival, and disappeared under a stone bridge that ran over a nearly dried-out creek.

After only the slightest of pauses, I followed. But the rabbit was gone. Spinning, I searched for a hole. A ninebark grew at the base of the bridge. I pulled back the branches and gasped. I'd heard stories about a network of underground tunnels that crisscrossed the country so that Angora Roux could safely make their deliveries, but I'd never known anyone who'd actually found one. Not that it mattered—humans supposedly couldn't enter them anyway.

This hole was very nearly my size. Curious, I reached out a hand. It slid easily into the dark. I hunched over and stepped forward. Then I crept forward again, stopping once I was entirely inside. The air was a great deal colder, more like late fall than the height of summer. A shiver raced through me as my sweat-drenched body struggled to acclimate. My eyes adjusted. The tunnel was nothing more than rough-cut walls with a hard-packed dirt floor. I was trying to decide whether to continue on when the dim light disappeared, cloaking me in an eerie darkness.

My stomach jumped to my throat. I whirled around and lunged for the exit. Where an opening had been moments before, there was now only solid earth. I flailed, searching for a way out. It was no use—I was trapped.

The cool air suddenly seemed thin and stale. I fought against my rising panic. Terrible images flooded my mind. I saw myself wandering the tunnels until I collapsed into an exhausted ball. Slowly starving to death. Disappearing without Maman ever knowing what'd become of me. Rabbits would hop by, doing nothing as the flesh rotted from my bones.

A faint thudding reached my ears. The skunk-rabbit! Careful to remain bent over so as not to bang my head, I began loping through the tunnel as fast as I could manage.

I ran with one hand in front of me and the other dragging along the ragged walls.

After several minutes, my heels began to sting. Terrific—blisters. I ripped off my tight-fitting shoes and started off again. Hours passed. My back first ached and then screamed in pain, but fear drove me forward. I never seemed to close the distance between me and the rabbit, but I never lost it, either. Every time I considered giving up, the thought of being trapped down here drove me on.

Eventually, a faint bit of light glinted in the distance. An exit!

I stumbled out of the tunnel, wincing as a branch from the bush guarding the entrance caught my hair. Out in the open, I slowly straightened, rubbing my lower back and breathing in the thick, muggy air. Though the sun had already started to sink over the horizon, the light burned my eyes.

After they adjusted, I saw I was standing in a vast meadow. The summer sun had crisped most of the grass, but evergreens towered overhead and the fresh scent of pine filled my nose. Birds chirped and squawked, understandably alarmed by my sudden appearance. There were no signs of the city—or civilization—anywhere.

Across the meadow, a black blur with a white streak hopped between two trees and vanished into thin air.

I sprang forward. A never-ending expanse of forest stretched out behind the two evergreens where I last saw the rabbit. When I crossed between the trees,

I shivered. The pressing heat disappeared, and the air suddenly felt different. Lighter. Cooler. But that wasn't the strangest part. The strangest part was that the forest had disappeared.

I now stood on the edge of a vast field. Rows of Chou de vie stretched in front of me. The small globes ranged from bright green to the dark purple of an eggplant. A sweet, milky scent filled the air.

Behind me, the space between the evergreens shimmered like a magical doorway visible only from this side. The world I'd come from could be seen only through the doorway, and even then it was faint, like the sun on that side had suddenly dimmed.

Filled with awe, I dropped to my knees in front of a globe that was still green but streaked with hints of reddish-purple. I'd seen Chou de vie in planters around the city, but I'd never encountered one up close. It was even more beautiful, more miraculous, than I ever could have imagined.

Slowly, hesitantly, I reached out. The leaves were velvety soft. Hardly daring to breathe, I rested a palm on the plant. It rose and fell as the baby inside took deep, relaxed breaths.

An actual baby!

The plant bulged. I imagined the baby stretching inside and giggled.

I clapped a hand over my mouth and glanced around.

Where were the rabbits?

I squinted, but the Warren was made up of little more than dark shadows now that day had slipped into night. Beyond the rows of Chou, I thought I made out a cluster of deciduous trees, but I couldn't be certain. I rubbed my forehead, suddenly aware of the predicament I'd landed myself in. I was far from home, and every inch of my body ached. There was no chance of making it back to Mignon tonight.

Again, I stroked the Chou. The smooth, rhythmic expansion and contraction of the plant was strangely soothing. I imagined parting the leaves and carefully lifting the infant into my arms. I could practically see a sweet girl peering up at me with soft brown eyes.

I'd feed her Lait de Chou and then goat milk until she was ready for mashed vegetables. I'd teach her to clap, to crawl, to walk. To talk.

I wanted to stay with the Chou until it ripened, but

I couldn't risk discovery by the rabbits. I had to go.

I knew this, but I couldn't make myself move, couldn't make myself pull my hand from the Chou I'd connected with, the Chou I'd already started to care for. Longing welled up inside me. There had to be hundreds—thousands—of Chou here. One more or less wouldn't matter to the rabbits either way. Not like it would matter to me. I wanted a little sister. *Needed* a little sister.

My hands reached for the ground as if acting on their own accord. I dug down in the rich soil around the Chou, loosening the dirt around the thick stem and long, delicate roots. Then I cradled the top of the Chou de vie, gently twisting it from the ground. It slid out without the slightest fuss.

It wants to come with me, I reassured myself. I lifted the outer fabric of my dress and wrapped it around the Chou, pulling it close to my chest.

"Welcome to the family, my petit Chou," I murmured.

And then I took off running.

Chapter Five: *Quincy*

I wish I could skip the next part of the story, but I wouldn't be much of a storyteller if I left out the embarrassing stuff. As we continue on, I beg you to keep in mind that even the greatest of heroes have their low moments. This happened to be one of mine.

I hopped happily across the Chou field, oblivious to the fact that I'd been followed, enamored with the bags of seeds nestled in my pouch (and even more thirsty than I was hungry, but that's neither here nor there).

My arrival was timed perfectly—everyone had retired to their burrows for the evening, leaving the field under the care of the watch rabbit, who greeted me from across the field.

The first few moments after I hopped in the burrow were even better than I'd hoped. My siblings were all cuddled together, listening to Maman tell a bedtime story.

"Good evening, greetings, good day," I said.

They looked up, startled. Maman sprang to her feet.

"Are you . . . are you a ghost?" Estelle said.

Sophie binkied. "'Course he's not a ghost!"

I breathed in deep, letting the musty scent of the cool den and the familiar smell of my many siblings wrap around me as Maman and the rest rushed toward me, flinging questions and comments every which way.

"Where've you been?"

"What happened?"

"We thought the fox got you for sure!"

"Glad you're back, cabbage-breath." (That last one was from Durrell.)

Maman broke through the chaos and rested her forehead against mine. "I thought I'd lost you."

I pulled back. "I'm sorry I worried you. But I had to go, and I knew you wouldn't let me if I asked first."

Maman's whiskers twitched as she switched into lecture mode. "What could possibly be worth your life? Quincy, have you lost your carrots? You could have been hurt or killed. Didn't the run-in with the fox teach you anything?"

"Oooh, Quincy's in trou-ble," Durrell said.

"Hush," Maman said, as Estelle nipped one of Durrell's ears.

"Maman, let me explain." I meant to sound like a hero, but my words came out as little more than a squeak.

"This better be good," Maman said.

I sucked in a deep breath. "Your whole life, you've farmed the Chou de vie so that humans could have their babies. And for what? Look at you, Maman. Your ribs are showing through your pelt."

As I continued, my voice grew stronger. More confident. "A half carrot isn't enough for any of us—we deserve more. And we'll never get it as long as we rely on humans for our food. That stops now."

My siblings' noses twitched as they waited for my big reveal.

I pulled the bags of seeds from my pouch.

"Quincy," Maman said. "Are those—"

I interrupted before I processed Maman's tired voice.

"Carrot seeds," I announced proudly.

The burrow echoed with the roar of my brothers and sisters cheering.

"We'll never go hungry again."

"I'm going to eat two carrots at every meal! Three, if I feel like it."

"We can cut back on the size of the Chou field!"

"We can stop farming Chou altogether!"

"STOP," Maman roared.

Silence fell over the burrow. Maman never yelled. Never.

She licked her paw and groomed her face before speaking.

"Quincy," she said tiredly. "I know your heart was in the right place, but did it never occur to you that we've tried growing our own carrots?"

"Pardon?"

Maman's gaze held no signs of pride. Her whiskers twitched.

"Carrots won't grow in the Warren," she said. "We've tried before—and failed."

"Then we'll try again," I said. "Maybe your seeds were bad. Maybe they didn't get enough hydration—"

"Maybe they were over-hydrated," Estelle said.

I threw her a grateful glance.

"We've tried again and again through the generations. The simple truth is that we can't grow our own carrots."

I shook my head, refusing to believe it. Maman was wrong—she had to be. "How come nobody ever told us this before? How come *you* never told us this before?"

She shook her head sadly. "It never occurred to me that you'd try something like this."

I hated the compassion in her eyes. The pity. I'd heard humans turned bright red when they were embarrassed; thankfully, my fur covered me so I didn't have to find out if the same held true for rabbits.

I wish I could say this was the lowest moment of my story. But you and I both know it gets worse. Much worse.

Because at that precise moment, the watch rabbit's thumping caught our attention. Three thumps followed by a pause and then three more. The call to assembly.

I perked my ears along with Maman and my siblings.

Maman left the den first. The rest of us trailed behind. The watch rabbit stood at the Warren's exit, his nose twitching with agitation.

The inhabitants of the closer dens had already gathered. Members of the Committee ensured everyone's attendance, then the eldest sat upright. Fosette's front paw was missing—a battle she'd fought with a hawk and nearly lost. (The Warren's healing magic is powerful, but it can't regrow missing limbs.)

"What's this about?" she asked.

The watch rabbit stepped aside, revealing a pile of disturbed dirt in the exact spot a Chou de vie should have been growing.

A gasp swept through the assembly.

"We had an intruder," the watch rabbit said.

"What kind of intruder?" Fosette asked.

"Did you get a look?" Chesney asked.

"How did the intruder get in?" someone called.

Fosette held up her paw. "One question at a time."

"It was a human," the watch rabbit said.

Again, we all gasped. A human in our Warren was unheard of and could only mean one thing. We'd been discovered.

"Why didn't you send up a signal the moment they entered?" Fosette asked.

"I didn't notice," the watch rabbit said, bowing his head.

"What were you doing if not watching the entrance?"

"I was doing my rounds over on the other side of the field. By the time I saw her, she was running for the exit."

Chesney hopped forward. "She?"

"Judging by the scent left behind, yes. And young, if I'm not mistaken."

No. My chest squeezed tight. The girl *had* followed me, but I'd lost her before I reached the garden. Besides, the tunnels were protected from humans the same way all the other creatures were kept out—with the magical door that only opened for Roux. (Sure, transport rabbits came back with occasional reports of mice or squirrels sneaking in behind them, but how was I supposed to know this might happen with something as large as a human?)

I panted as I replayed the journey in my mind. There had been some noises in the tunnel, but I'd been so anxious to return that they hadn't really registered. I suppose I'd chalked them up to sounds filtering in from the human world.

The truth crept through me, raising my body temperature.

I opened my mouth, trying to release some of the heat.[9] This was bad. This was very, very bad. I was tempted to start digging my own burrow so that I could sink into the ground and disappear. Instead, I slowly edged backward, hoping nobody noticed my retreat.

"What are we going to do?" someone shouted.

"The Committee will convene immediately. Until a decision is reached, it's business as usual."

"That's a pile of rotten carrots," someone yelled.

"I say we strike until the Chou is returned," Durrell shouted.

---

9. *Rabbits don't have sweat glands all over like humans—ours are located in our mouths. But they are small, and even panting isn't very helpful at regulating our temperatures.*

The air filled with frantic chatter. My gaze landed on Maman, on her wide eyes, her twitching nose. I hung my head. I couldn't stand knowing that I was the source of her pain, that I'd put the Warren in danger. I took off for the exit.

Before I passed through the evergreens, I checked behind me. As usual, no one even noticed that I'd slipped away. For the first time, I was glad to be invisible. Hopefully that would hold long enough for me to fix the terrible mess I'd created.

Chapter Six: *Fleurine*

I didn't think of it as stealing the Chou, not as I clutched it to my chest, not as I raced from the Warren, not as I crossed the meadow. Not when I stopped in front of the bush guarding the tunnel's entrance. My only thought was returning home, planting the Chou, and waiting to meet my sister. (I may have had one other thought as well: how much more quickly I'd be able to move if I hadn't discarded my shoes. My bare feet throbbed, making each step torture.)

I pushed aside the bush and blinked. A grassy slope greeted me. I spun, thinking perhaps I was at the wrong spot. But no, I was standing right where I'd exited the tunnel—I was sure of it. The entrance had disappeared. I swallowed, but it had been hours since my last sip of water. My throat was dry and scratchy, and my head felt fuzzy, like my brain had dried out along with the rest of my body. Thoughts buzzed around like pesky flies, but there was nothing I could catch, nothing I could turn into a solid plan. How was I to get home?

A bat swooped over my head. The baby inside the Chou squirmed, reminding me that I had more than myself to think about. Montpeyroux wasn't all that large—surely, there'd be a road or a village nearby where I could seek help.

A break in the foliage revealed a path. Bright moonlight exposed a heart-shaped print. My grip on the Chou tightened. Where there were deer, there were also lynx and wolves. But I couldn't very well wait around for morning—at some point, the Roux would discover the missing Chou, and I had no idea if they'd go searching for it when they did. Velvety darkness wrapped around us as I stumbled along the trail. Shadowed branches reached out, attempting to claw my face.

I shifted the Chou to one arm and walked with the other out in front, but I soon had to switch. Before

long, both arms, unaccustomed to carrying anything for any distance, quivered worse than my
already exhausted legs. I carefully set down the
Chou, stepped out of one of my petticoats, and used
it to fashion a makeshift cradle over my shoulder.

The Chou's roots were drier than I would have
liked. It'd been years since I'd helped Jean-André
transplant anything in the garden, and I couldn't
remember how long a plant could survive out of the
soil without going into shock, but he'd said it was
important not to let the roots dry out completely.
"Hold on," I whispered. "We'll be home soon."

I didn't know if it was true, but I needed to believe
it—for my sister's sake and my own. Even though
she'd only just entered my life, she'd already planted
herself in my heart, a tiny seed of hope and wonder.

I'd never been alone in the woods before, much
less at night. On any other occasion, the hoots and
scratching around me might have been a welcome
change from the noise of the city. Tonight, every
crack and chirp threatened danger—or at least discovery. I half-expected a rabbit to jump out in front of
me as I rounded each bend.

I'd only just determined to take a break when the roar of a river reached me. I followed the sound until I reached the edge of the treeline. Rushing water glistened in the moonlight.

I pushed aside a bush and picked my way down the steep, rocky bank, slipping a little. At the bottom I adjusted the Chou and bent to lift a handful of cool water to my mouth. It took some time to drink my fill, but with each drop, my confidence and strength returned. I opened the sling and moistened the Chou's roots, taking care not to wash the soil away. "We'll be home soon," I whispered again.

I settled on a large boulder and slid my throbbing feet into the refreshing water, nearly groaning with relief.

A series of slick stones stretched across the river. After only a short rest, I forced myself to leap across, teetering and nearly losing my balance on a particularly small rock right in the center. On the other side, I found a break in the shrubs. The winding trail eventually widened into an open field filled with tall, feathery stalks of barley. *Thank the rabbits!* Where there were crops, there were surely people. I threaded my way through the field until I reached a wide, worn road.

I hesitated before starting for the city, hoping I hadn't gotten turned around in the woods. But Maman always said that indecision marked a weak leader. She was right—the surest way never to make it home would be to sit perfectly still. I set off, walking at a determined pace despite the rocks pressing into my tender feet.

More than an hour passed, and I didn't encounter so much as a cottage where I might find relief. Finally, my shaking legs refused to carry me one more step. I waded through the tall grasses on the side of the road, tucked myself under the limbs of a graceful oak, and fell into a restless sleep plagued by horrible dreams.

In one, I pulled up my crop of purple carrots only to find that they were all black and coated in thick slime. In another, I was standing at the entrance to the Montpeyroux Académie of Science, but I couldn't go in unless I gave up my Chou de vie. Later, I was surrounded by a pack of rabid rabbits, all demanding that I tell them the name of the botanical family the Chou belonged to. Every time I opened my mouth, a high-pitched squeak came out. I was forced to stand to the side as a long row of rabbits hopped through the Académie's doors.

The first rays of morning sun woke me. Or was it the clomp, clomp, clomping of a horse coming down the lane? I sprang to my feet, groggy from far too little sleep but determined not to miss my first chance at rescue. I peeked at the Chou resting quietly at my chest. My heart flooded with warmth as I imagined parting the leaves and lifting my sister in my arms.

A wagon came slowly into view, silhouetted by the rising sun. It was headed in the direction I'd come from the night before, but I waved it to a stop. A stick-thin boy about my age, with suntanned skin and big ears only partially hidden under a straw hat, perched in the seat, reins in hand. His coarsely woven tunic was spotted with clumsy patches. The back of the wagon was covered with a bulging canvas, concealing what I guessed must be recently harvested grains.

"Help you, Miss?" His blue eyes—the color of delphiniums—were bright and curious.

"I'm looking for Mignon."

"Looking the wrong way, far as I can tell."

I stifled a groan. Maybe there were things worse than indecision, at least when it came to being lost in the woods.

"What are you doing out here by yourself, anyway?" the boy asked.

He spoke in a manner typical of country folk— slower, with a nasally vowel pronunciation that made him difficult to understand. The edges of his lips were turned up slightly.

"My sister and I were out for a walk and got lost." I motioned to the lump at my chest, hoping he'd believe it was a slumbering toddler.

"You can hitch a ride back to the city with me." He started to exit the wagon. "Let me give you a hand."

"No," I said quickly, "I'm quite all right." I was glad for the ride, but the last thing I needed was him getting any closer to the Chou than necessary.

I hurried around the wagon, taking care to hide my bare feet, and pulled myself awkwardly up to the seat beside him. The horse directly in front of me lifted its tail and dropped a pile of smelly dung on the road.

The boy urged the horses forward. "You been out all night?"

Instead of answering, I asked, "How long until we reach Mignon?"

"Two hours to the gates."

I squeezed the Chou, wishing I could meet my new sister now.

"You must be thirsty," the boy said. He passed me a worn leather flask. After a moment's hesitation, I uncorked it and took a long, deep swig. I choked, spewing a sour, yeasty liquid from my mouth.

The boy cast a sideways glance. "Not used to drinking ale?"

"Swallowed wrong is all." I forced myself to take another drink, then returned the flask.

He studied me with renewed curiosity. I twisted my ring so the coat of arms wasn't visible and cursed the lace on my dress. The less anyone knew about where I'd been or who I was, the better. Especially once Maman turned up with a new daughter.

"What's your name?" I asked, hoping to draw his attention away from me.

"Ignace," he said. "Yours?"

"Fleur—Flo," I said, catching myself.

"You live in the city?"

"I do."

"What were you doing walking all the way out here?"

"We were picnicking in the woods when we wandered away from the carriage and got turned around. Maman and Papá must be ever so worried." I didn't have a papá, of course—Maman never married. But I was quite proud of adding that last bit in, certain it would throw the boy off my scent.

"Won't they still be looking for you?"

Uh-oh. "I'm certain they'll return home to round up a search party. I'll meet them there."

"You don't have to worry," he said. "I'll have you home in no time."

"What are you going to the city for?"

"Dropping off this load and picking up more seed."

That caught my interest. "What kind of seed?"

"Lentil."

I jerked my head toward the bed of the wagon. "That's what you're hauling?"

"This is wheat."

"Crop rotation." The words slipped out before I could think otherwise.

His eyebrows jumped.

Now the edges of my lips turned up. "Living in the city doesn't mean I don't know a thing or two about farming."

"I guess I never expected those fancy schools of yours to teach farming."

"They don't," I said. "It's a hobby."

"A hobby?"

"You know, something to do for fun."

"I know what a hobby is. I'm surprised anyone would find farming fun."

His calloused hands snapped the reins as he urged the horses to pick up the pace.

"Well, not farming exactly, but botany—the seeds and the plants themselves. I'd love to understand how it all works."

"Spend a day on the farm and you'll see pretty quickly that there isn't much to it. You plant the seeds, hope the weather cooperates, and harvest when the time comes."

I was starting to get used to the way words rolled from his mouth smooth and slow, like honey from a bottle. But I couldn't believe he didn't think farming was fascinating.

"What about crop rotation?" I asked.

"What about it?"

"Why do you do it?"

"Because it produces healthier crops."

"Yes, but why?"

He shrugged. "Never spent much time thinking about it, truth be told."

"I think about it all the time. Why do different crops grow in different climates? Different soil? Why do they grow at all? How does one tiny seed grow into a plant? Is there something in the soil that feeds them? Why do they need water and sunshine?"

"Seems like a waste of time to me. You plant the seeds. They grow. End of story."

"You're not even the slightest bit curious about it all?"

He shifted in his seat. "This hobby of yours is fine for rich city folk, but people like me, we don't sit around with our heads buried in books. My days start with hard work and don't end until it's done. That's the way it is, and that's the way it'll always be."

His words were more sad than bitter.

"Do something else," I said. "Go to school. Study a trade."

He snorted. "You have no idea how the real world works, do you?"

I lifted my chin. "I do so."

"There's a reason my parents have fourteen children—they need every one of us to help on the farm."

"You have *thirteen* brothers and sisters?"

I'd heard farmers often had enormous families to help with all the work, but I'd never known anyone with a family that size. Fourteen bundles of carrots would have cost a pretty penny before—what would happen to farmers now that purple carrots had become so expensive? Maybe they'd all start trying to grow their own. I knew firsthand how hard that was, but at least they had the land they'd need.

"Should be fifteen," Ignace said. "Two never made it out of the cradle."

Although babies were always healthy to start, they were often lost to sicknesses before they were old enough to walk. I tightened my arms around the Chou. This baby would make it. I'd see to that.

One of the horses neighed and flicked its tail. As Ignace soothed it, I tried to imagine having thirteen brothers and sisters. "Are you the oldest or youngest?"

He lowered the reins to his knee. "You always ask this many questions?"

"Only when I want answers. Oldest or youngest?"

"Third oldest. You?"

"Only chi—" I scrambled to correct my mistake. "Only the two of us," I said, patting the Chou.

Ignace narrowed his eyes so I raced to change the subject. "What would you do if you could do anything?"

"Never thought about it."

He said it so fast that I suspected it wasn't quite true. "There must be something you dream of?"

The wagon wheels crunched and the horses' hooves clomped against the hard-packed road. "I suppose I'd like to try my hand at sailing."

I blinked. "Sailing?"

"I can't even imagine a body of water that stretches out farther than our fields, farther than the eye can see. I wouldn't mind exploring the Seven Seas, traveling where the winds carried me."

I'd been all over Montpeyroux with Maman, but the only time she'd left the country was on a diplomatic trip to Gatineau, and I'd remained safely at home. It was bad enough that the citizens carried dead rabbits' feet around in their pockets for luck, but the country was also plagued by Voyants who apparently came up from a frightening place they called the Bog, bringing with them invisible Great White Wolves and certain death.

I shuddered, unable to imagine actually wanting to leave the safety of Montpeyroux. Then again, sailing off on the Seven Seas might be this boy's only chance at freedom. That was something I understood all too well. I cradled the Chou. Once I had a sibling, Maman wouldn't be so focused on me all the time.

My stomach rumbled.

Holding the reins in one hand, the boy—Ignace— used the other to dig in a burlap bag at his feet. When he sat up, he passed me a biscuit. It was harder than the ones Bernadette made, but I was in no position to refuse food.

My head buzzed with questions while I tried to work up enough saliva to swallow, but now that I was safely on my way back to the city, the steady clopping of the horses' hooves slowed my thoughts, pulling my eyelids down over my eyes.

This time when I slept, my dreams turned to the field of Chou de vie. In the first, Maman helped me harvest a leaf to study under a microscope. In the next, all the Chou ripened at the same time, and I raced from one plant to another, attempting to gather all the babies in my arms. In my final dream, I was accepting an award for my contributions to understanding the science behind the Chou de vie when an army of rabbits interrupted and began attacking us with crude spears.

I woke with a startled gasp, wondering for the briefest of eternities why I was in a wagon at Mignon's gates. Memories of the previous night flooded back to me. I realized my makeshift sling had shifted while I slept, revealing a small patch of leaf. I tugged at the fabric, hoping Ignace hadn't seen the Chou.

Luckily, he was focused on controlling the anxious horses. It was midmorning and the road leading in and out of Mignon was crammed with travelers, some arriving to shop or trade wares, others departing. I suspected it was extra busy due to the traffic from the Summer Festival. The horses tossed back their heads and neighed as if begging to turn around and go home. When their pleas went unanswered, their tails swished with anger.

I tensed as we rolled up to the gates. To my immense relief, the guard waved us through without so much as a second glance. Ignace turned the wagon toward the granary.

"Thank you for the ride," I said. "Right here will be fine."

He pulled the wagon to a stop in front of a bakery. The smell of chocolate-filled croissants made my mouth water.

"You sure you and your *sister*"—the way he emphasized *sister* made me think he'd seen more than I hoped as I slept—"don't need a ride home?"

"Very sure." I climbed down from the wagon, wincing when I landed on my sore feet. "Thank you."

I wished I had a bag of coins to offer, but my gratitude would have to suffice. "Your kindness won't be forgotten."

He nodded a silent goodbye. I felt his gaze follow me as I pulled the Chou closer and hurried toward home. An ache filled my chest, one I couldn't quite explain. In different circumstances, Ignace and I might have been friends. I would have liked to learn more about his life, about farming tricks and techniques. About his enormous family. Something about the boy reminded me of a closed-up daisy, but I had a feeling he needed more than sunshine to bloom.

The guard at our front gate bowed deferentially upon my arrival, but his wide eyes told me I was in an even worse state than I'd imagined. Indeed, I was still carrying the Chou wrapped in my petticoat. My dress was dirty and torn, and my hair had slipped from my updo. I expected to be recognized, but people either looked right through me or wrinkled their noses and looked away. I wondered how many times I'd done the same to strangers I'd passed on the street.

Though my parched throat screamed for water, I hurried around the house and through the gardens, dropping to my knees when I finally reached my plantings hidden in the corner. I set the Chou aside and began scooping out soil with my bare hands. Once I'd created a big enough hole, I tenderly picked the Chou up and cradled it in my arms.

"I told you I'd take care of you," I murmured, smiling when my sister rewarded me with the smallest of wiggles. I began lowering the Chou into the ground. The roots seemed to stretch and strain, reaching for the earth as if sensing that's where it belonged.

A caterpillar crawled along the thick stem of a nearby gourd, heading for a leaf. The rest of the plant's leaves were already chewed. I froze. What if the caterpillar—or anything else—chewed the Chou's leaves? Would that destroy it? Prevent it from ripening? I glanced back to the house. The Chou wouldn't be visible from my bedroom. Normally, a Chou bonne would be called in to sit with a transplanted Chou until it was ready for harvest, but I couldn't very well hope to keep my secret with a nurse sitting here.

I straightened, pulling the Chou to my chest as my mind raced. I couldn't plant it here. And if I planted it in the garden, Jean-André would find it. Same with the housemaids if I tried to keep it in a planter in my quarters.

That only left one option. I wrapped the Chou back in my skirt and raced for the house. Elodie was in the servants' dining room, humming as she altered a dress Maman thought fit me a little too snugly.

When I burst in, she jumped to her feet and curtsied, her eyes wide with surprise.

"When you didn't show up for any of your commitments, I thought there'd been a mix-up and that you went off with your maman!"

My eyebrows pulled together as I tried to figure out what she was talking about. Right. Maman left yesterday on a trip; I was to have made all sorts of appearances for the festival. "Oh, um, yes. I went along for the first little bit, but it was so dull I decided to come home early."

Though Maman would be as mad as a wet rabbit when she learned of my absence, I was pleased a temporary explanation for where I'd been had dropped itself in my lap.

But Elodie's eyes narrowed as she took in my disheveled appearance and bare feet. "What in the cabbage patch happened to you?"

Her gaze came to rest on the bundle in my arms.

"I'll explain later. Right now, we need to depart for the cottage."

"The cottage?"

"That's right," I said. "We're leaving immediately."

"But we're not packed. They won't be expecting us. And it's the Summer Festival! Besides, my maman, she won't have—"

"We'll send a footman to notify your maman. We'll only be away a night or two."

A Chou bonne had been at one of Maman's parties recently, and I'd overheard her say that Chou always ripen within a couple days of delivery.

"But my maman, she—"

I couldn't believe Elodie was arguing. I drew myself up and spoke in a firm voice, as I'd seen Maman do so many times. "Please have the carriage brought around. Pack whatever you can in the meantime."

Elodie rearranged her face into a bland expression.

I softened my tone. "I'll ask Bernadette to prepare us a basket."

She dropped into a curtsey. "Yes, Miss."

I breathed a sigh of relief. Showing up alone at the cottage would draw more attention than I wanted.

A short time later, I'd quenched my thirst, changed into a fresh dress, transferred the Chou to a large silk scarf, watered the roots, and secured a basket from Bernadette. Our driver helped me into our personal carriage, which was much cozier than the ceremonial carriage I'd taken with Maman yesterday. Elodie stepped up behind me. I tugged the heavy curtains shut and rested against the generously cushioned seat back.

"Are you going to tell me what this is all about?" Elodie asked.

I longed to tell her the truth, but I didn't know if she could be trusted. This was too big. Too important. "It's nothing," I said. "I only felt like a bit of fresh air."

She glared at the bundle in my arms. "If it's nothing, how do you explain *that*?"

The sage-colored silk scarf covering the Chou had slipped, revealing the Chou's purple-tinged leaves.

My mouth went dry as I scrambled for an explanation. This was bad. This was very, very bad.

Chapter Seven: *Quincy*

My ears worked overtime, and my nose twitched as I darted about the meadow. The girl's odor, unmistakably onion mixed with a heavy dose of lavender, had led me directly to the tunnel and then disappeared. I couldn't detect any unusual sounds from the woods, but I finally picked up her trail again near a break in the shrubs. I hurried along the path as fast as my aching legs allowed, not bothering to avoid the leaves and needles that crunched under my paws, alerting the woods to my presence.

A branch cracked on the trail ahead. I rushed around a bend, expecting to spot the girl, and skidded to a stop. An enormous four-legged creature towered above me. A deer. I'd seen one before, grazing in the meadow when we went out foraging. Maman said they were gentle creatures, but I veered off the path, unwilling to risk passing too close. Its legs were spindly, but the antlers spiking from its head looked as though they could inflict serious damage.

The deer plucked a leaf from a branch and chewed. Its wide, serious eyes followed me as I found my way back to the trail.

Lucky thing, roaming the country at its leisure. Not having to cower and hide from every predator in the woods, not having to prove itself to anyone.

I sniffed the air. It had been some time since I detected the girl's scent. Worried that I'd lost her, I climbed a hill, rounded a bend, and found myself in front of something larger than a creek. It almost certainly wasn't Angora Gorge, which Maman said was made when an Angora Rex got angry that a patch of forest had been cleared by humans. He thumped his foot so hard that the earth cracked clean in half, forming a deep gorge that later filled with water. But this one was wider, and deeper, than the creek back home. And flowing plenty fast enough to sweep me away to who knows where.

I scoured the bank and found the girl's scent down near the water. She must have crossed. Maman said that Great Maman Rabbit had gifted all rabbits the ability to swim, but that wasn't a theory I was eager to test. (Especially because we'd never been allowed to swim in the creek at the Warren for fear the current might sweep us away.) A series of rocks jutted out above the water, but the gaps between some of them were enormous. Even if I made the jump, the stones were almost certainly slippery.

Yet there was no choice, not if I wanted the Chou back. I took a deep breath and tightened my muscles, preparing to leap.

Sticks cracked in the bushes above.

I spun around. My brother towered above me. "Durrell!"

"Quincy, what are you doing?"

I remained tightly wound. "I'm—nothing."

Durrell was the last one I could tell about the girl.

"Looks like something to me."

"What are you doing here?" I asked.

"Looking for you."

"Me? What for?"

"I saw you slip out of the Warren. Thought you might know something about the missing Chou. It's strange that it happened right after you returned, don't you think?"

I gulped. "Does Maman know I'm gone again?"

"I'm sure she does by now."

"I'm not coming back. Not without the Chou."

"Quincy, don't be a cottontail. It's dangerous out here. Come on. We need to get back to the Warren."

"No."

"It's not a choice."

Our gazes locked. Durrell's eyes were hard, unrelenting. If he wanted me, he was going to have to catch me.

I spun around, regained my balance, and sprang for the first rock, a small island thrusting up from the whirling water. My aim was true, and I landed in the center of the stone, using it to leap for the next. This one was smaller, trickier. The surface sloped, making the water splash up against it before parting and flowing around either side. I landed on my back paws and nearly overshot before regaining my balance and jumping again.

The water swirled under me, roaring with hunger.

The next rock was small but smooth and flat. I would have made it, if only I hadn't miscalculated the distance. Or maybe it was my legs giving out. Either way, my front paws made contact with the stone a moment before the rest of my body crashed into the river. The swift current pulled me under.

Cold water filled my mouth. I flailed, seeking purchase on something, anything, that might save me. There was nothing. I kicked furiously and broke through the surface, gasping for air. "Durrell," I yelled. "Durrell, help!"

But the river had already swept me down and away, far from my brother's reach.

The bank. I had to make it to the bank. The harder I paddled, the harder the creek battled. The current picked up and a loud roar filled my ears. The next time my head popped above the water, I strained to see in front of me. The angry river rushed ahead, then disappeared.

Estelle once told me about a place where water poured over a cliff taller than a tree, about the thundering sound that filled her ears as it crashed into a pool far below.

I paddled furiously, willing myself toward the shore. It was no use. The roar grew louder, the water more ferocious. And then I was dropping. Dropping, dropping, dropping through the air. My stomach left my body. This was it—my final moments alive. I would die alone, the Warren's last memory of me that I'd betrayed them. Exposed them.

I'm sorry, I wanted to cry out.

The world exploded around me and I found myself being pulled to and from, tossed and turned under the water as if I were a mere leaf blowing in the wind. My lungs ached. I kicked and fought. *Please, Great Maman Rabbit, save me,* I begged.

I broke through the surface a single twitch before I gasped for air.

A small log bumped against me. I cradled it under my chin, using it to help me stay afloat. The river carried me downstream, sweeping me under what could only be the Golden Carrot Bridge (named for the statues that stood guard on either end) and past a series of floating vessels with humans swarming about. Mignon! Instinct kicked in and I paddled furiously, but every time I attempted to reach the bank, a fierce current sucked me back to the middle of the river.

The city had long since disappeared when my foot finally caught on something solid. I scrambled up the bank and used my last bit of energy to fling myself on the shore. I wanted to collapse, but Maman said carnivores usually came out at night. And even though we were tough and stringy, there were any number of animals willing to give us a try.

I hopped under the arms of a small bush, my body trembling uncontrollably as my mind struggled to process the magnitude of my failure. I'd lost the girl and gotten myself lost in the process. Now I'd never find her in time to rescue the Chou before it started to rot—never redeem myself in Maman's eyes. I couldn't bear the thought of returning to the Warren with empty paws. My siblings would torment me, reminding me day in and day out of my failure. Instead of skunk or cabbage-breath, they'd start calling me worthless.

Worthless, worthless, worthless, their voices echoed in my head. Finally, the tremors subsided and I was blanketed by a fatigue so heavy it was impossible to fight. At least a predator would find some use for me, which was more than I could say for the Warren.

I startled awake and tensed my muscles. Though I was groggy and more than a little sore, I was also ready to bolt if necessary. A songbird chirped overhead, and the warm morning air carried no hint of danger. That didn't mean I was safe. I longed to return to the Warren, but I had a job to do. If I followed the river upstream, I'd make my way back to Mignon. With any luck, I'd also find the girl.

After taking care of my morning business (which included even fewer cecotropes than I was used to on account of the lack of food the day before), I took a few moments to nibble on a small patch of green clover, trying to convince myself that the bland roughage was a delicious purple carrot. When I'd had all I could take, I sprang into motion, ignoring the complaints of my tired, bruised body and my unhappy stomach.

If only I were back in our burrow—even half a carrot would be better than nothing. I wondered who helped Maman distribute them in my absence. Thinking of the burrow made me think about

Durrell. By now, he'd certainly alerted Maman to the debacle[10] at the river, which meant she'd be worried sick. My stomach twisted again, this time from more than discomfort.

I followed the river upstream, growing ever more hopeful as the woods thinned and finally parted, revealing the floating vessels I'd passed earlier. My ears guided me to the roar of the city. I soon encountered a busy road teeming with carriages, horses, and wagons passing in and out of an arch in the tallest wall I'd ever seen. The arched entrance of Mignon!

Forgetting my aching muscles and bruised paws, I rushed ahead, darting in and around the many legs and wheels that clogged the way. Inside the city, I tucked into a corner and took my bearings. Now that I was here, I had no idea how to find the girl. Carriages groaned and creaked. Horses neighed. Voices rose and fell. Machinery clanked. The ruckus of what was apparently normal city life swirled inside my head.

Think, I told myself, trying to block out the noise. *Start with what you know*. The girl lived in

---

10. *It was bad enough that I'd embarrassed myself; why did it have to be in front of him?*

an impressive home near a garden, nothing like the small, dingy buildings around me. And her clean street had been nearly empty. This manure-spotted street buzzed with activity. I was definitely in the wrong area.

As I plotted my next move, a woman caught my attention. She held a basket in the crook of her arm. Her dress was full and round and adorned with more frills and bows than the rest of the crowd, but that wasn't what made her stand out. It was her smell. Onion and lavender—exactly like the girl.

I followed the woman at a distance. After several twists and turns, the narrow, noisy streets widened. The flurry of people and wagons gave way to carriages rolling leisurely through the streets. The odoriferous air changed to something lighter and fresher, something more natural.

I was starting to think this woman would lead me right to the girl when she paused on the stoop of an enormous but unfamiliar home and knocked several times on the door, which featured a carving of an Angora Rex. Their likenesses were all over the city—giant statues in front of buildings, rabbit silhouettes etched in the windows.

The rabbits were big and strong, but also fluffy and somehow cute. Did humans know the Angora Rex were gone, that they'd been replaced by the much smaller, and not nearly as cute, Angora Roux? I couldn't imagine the city filled with images of us.

My ears lay back against my head. If they gave us more carrots, we wouldn't look so terrible.

The door opened and the lady disappeared inside.

My hope deflated.

It'd been silly to think the woman—a perfect stranger—might lead me to the girl in the first place.

But I'd come this far—I couldn't quit now. I sat up on my hind legs and sniffed. At first, I was overwhelmed by the plethora[11] of scents that clogged the air, and I longed for the fresh smell of the Warren. But underneath it all, I detected the faint scent of pine trees. Of meadows. Of water. The garden!

I followed my nose until I found myself across the street from the very same rock wall that I'd encountered on my first visit. My heart raced. I'd done it! I'd found the girl's home! Or very nearly, anyway. This

---

11. *Maman says I sound pretentious when I use this word, but it's one of my favorites.*

street wasn't familiar, so I hopped along the wall, rounded a corner, and spotted the arched exit across from the girl's house.

I tucked myself into the shadows and studied the street. Carriages clopped by and humans made their way here and there. The horrid dog that had chased me the day before was nowhere to be seen.

I gathered my courage. The wide gates of the house swung open with a creak. Sensing my chance, I darted into the street. A carriage emerged, led by two magnificent black horses. Someone tugged the curtains closed, but not before I caught a glimpse of a face.

The face of the girl who had spotted me in the garden.

With a series of long jumps I didn't think my tired legs were capable of, I launched myself onto a platform at the back of the carriage.

Assuming she still had the Chou, it was as good as mine.

Chapter Eight: *Fleurine*

I shifted back on the seat and tugged the scarf over the Chou, hiding it from Elodie's accusing gaze.

"It's nothing," I said.

She didn't press me, but her judgment clouded the air like a thick, heavy fog as we left the noise of the city behind.

The curtains I'd closed only minutes earlier suddenly made the carriage feel like a prison. I yanked them open and readjusted the shawl so the Chou could enjoy a bit of sun while I inspected its leaves for signs that the reddish-purple streaks had darkened. I squinted. Was it me, or were the leaves ever-so-slightly wilted?

I wiped my suddenly clammy hands on my skirt,

remembering how I'd once started a cucumber vine in a bowl. When it grew larger than expected, I'd tried to plant it outside. But it had never really taken, and it shriveled and died soon after.

Horror filled my throat, making it so I could hardly swallow. I'd been careful to keep the Chou's roots damp. Once it was back in the earth, it'd recover. It had to.

We bumped down the road avoiding each other's gaze.

At least an hour passed before Elodie broke the silence. "What are your plans?"

"Pardon?"

She jerked her chin toward the Chou. "You're obviously determined to see this through. How are you going to keep it secret?"

"I mean to plant it in the corner of the garden. The leaves have already started turning—it won't be long before it's ready for harvest."

Elodie raised both eyebrows. "You're not expecting me to look after it?"

"Of course not." She wasn't a Chou bonne, and anyway, I didn't intend to let it out of my sight.

"And the baby?"

"What of it?"

"How are you going to explain prancing home with an infant in your arms?"

"Right now, I need to focus on planting the Chou. I'll figure everything else out after."

Outside, soaring trees (mostly *Acer platanoides*, though I spotted *Acer pseudoplatanus* as well—both members of the Sapindaceae family) came into view and then slowly disappeared.

"Why are you doing this?" Elodie's voice was softer. Inquisitive instead of disapproving.

Tears welled in my eyes. "I need this baby," I said. "I need a sister."

"A sister?" The surprise in Elodie's voice matched the surprise on her face. "You're doing all this for a *sister*?"

"You don't know what it's like." I swiped at the drop that forced its way over my eyelashes and down my cheek. "I'm so tired of being alone. Of trying to make Maman happy. Never having anyone to talk to."

"Your social card is always full!"

The skin under my ring suddenly itched. I didn't

know how to explain that I was always the loneliest when I was surrounded by people.

"Anyway," she said, "your maman is never going to agree."

"Maybe you should focus on doing your job and let me worry about this."

Elodie pressed her lips together.

Guilt pinched my stomach, but I couldn't force out an apology. No matter what happened with this Chou, Elodie would return home to her family. To her sisters. They didn't look alike—not like families in the plant world with their similar stems or leaves or blossoms—but the girls shared an invisible bond that I longed to share with someone.

We rode in silence until she pulled out our lunch of sausage, cheese, soft rolls, and blueberry tarts. She held out a small plate without meeting my gaze.

Though I was starving, I had to force myself to eat in between stealing peeks at the Chou. It seemed to be holding up. If only I knew how long it could survive being out of the ground. The roll sat in my stomach like a bag of rocks. I nibbled on the blueberry tart, but the normally delicious treat only made me nauseous. I handed the half-full plate back to Elodie, who returned the uneaten food to the basket.

Sharp silence cut the air as the miles passed. About the time my patience started to give way, a sprawling, three-story mansion came into view. It was framed by strategically planted trees, making it appear even more magnificent than it already was. (I had no idea why we called it a cottage, given that it was bigger than our home in the city.)

"I suppose you'll be going straight around the back?" Elodie's voice dripped with feigned politeness.

"Yes," I said. "Please see that we're settled. And not a word about this. To anyone."

I searched her face for some understanding, some recognition that I was doing what I had to, but she'd drawn a studiously deferential mask over her features. I squeezed the Chou. It didn't matter what Elodie thought—I was doing the right thing.

Pounding hooves drew our attention to the window. A horse overtook our carriage and then disappeared in front of us. I pressed my nose against the glass. "What in the carrots?"

"What is it?" Elodie asked.

"I'm not sure." I tucked the fabric around the Chou to cover it completely.

The carriage stopped in front of the cottage's imposing entrance. I flung open the door before the driver had a chance and climbed down to find Madame Faucon waiting. Almost a full head shorter than me, the housekeeper was a tiny woman who, like Maman, prized decorum above all else. Today, her cap was askew. Wrinkles crisscrossed her shawl and her flaxen face twisted into a frown. She curtseyed. "Miss Fleurine, thank heavens you arrived. But how did your maman find out so fast?"

I forced myself not to wrinkle my nose at her familiar scent. I'd asked her once, and she'd said it was daisy perfume, but it smelled to me of something closer to manure. "Find what out?"

She peered into the carriage. "Wherever is the Grande Lumière?" Her eyebrows pulled together as she turned back to me and noted the bundle in my arms. "What are you carrying?"

I cradled the Chou close. "Maman is away on business, and I needed some fresh air. These are plantings for the garden."

"Away on business—you mean she hasn't heard?"

"Heard what?"

Madame Faucon wrung her hands. An unfamiliar carriage was stopped in front of ours. The horse we'd seen rush by earlier was tied to a nearby tree, no rider in sight.

"I don't know if it's my place to say," Madame Faucon said.

"What?" I asked, impatient to get on with my task.

"It's the Toussaint family."

The Toussaints were a young couple that had recently purchased a cottage down the road. Maman invited them over for tea the last time we were here, and they'd seemed lovely.

I frowned, feeling a prickle of unease. "What of them? What's happened?"

"They left out a bundle of purple carrots last night and . . ."

"What?"

Madame Faucon leaned forward and lowered her voice. "The carrots were still there this morning."

I couldn't make sense of what I was hearing. "You can't mean a Chou wasn't delivered?"

Madame Faucon continued worrying her hands. "I sent word to your maman straight away. Apparently the Toussaints aren't the only ones."

"*No* Chou were delivered last night?" My unease blossomed into horror.

"Some deliveries were made," she said, "but not all of them."

She continued on, babbling anxiously about whether this was a sign of things to come, about the trouble we'd be in if the rabbits stopped delivering altogether. Her words garbled in my brain. This had never happened before in the entire history of Mignon. Chou were always delivered when a bundle of purple carrots was left out. Always.

Elodie's gaze pierced me from the dark of the carriage.

I gripped my Chou. This couldn't have anything to do with me. There'd been an entire field, and I'd only taken one small plant. A plant that I desperately needed to get into the ground.

Madame Faucon had stopped talking and was obviously waiting for my response.

If Maman were here, she'd have words of comfort

to offer and instructions to issue. She always said the most important task a leader had was to reassure the country in times of need.

I rubbed my thumb against my ring, searching for words of inspiration. "I'm . . . I'm sure Maman will return straightaway when she hears of this and get it sorted out."

Madame Faucon pursed her lips. "I hope you're right."

She straightened and attempted to draw her normally impervious cloak of judgment about her, but her hands were shaking.

My mind swirled like water in an eddy as I tried to work out some kind of solution. But even if what Madame Faucon was saying was true, even if there was an issue with the deliveries, there was nothing I could do about it.

The Chou squirmed, reminding me to focus. "Elodie will get us settled. I'm going to get these plants into the ground before they go into shock."

I started for the garden. A peek over my shoulder revealed Elodie climbing down from the carriage and giving directions for the little luggage we'd managed to assemble before our hasty departure.

I forced myself to maintain a leisurely pace until I rounded the corner, then I sped up, moving as quickly as I dared without jostling the Chou. "There, you see," I murmured. "I told you it wouldn't be long."

Birds chirped overhead, their cheerful song dissolving the hard knot in my chest. Maman could handle whatever was going on with the deliveries. And soon, I'd have a sister.

I moved along the edge of the sprawling lawn at the back of the cottage, careful not to trample the tempest's lace growing along the border. Although it was a wildflower, the feathery greens and soft clusters of delicate blooms were prized throughout the country for their beauty.

The lawn sloped down toward a pond. Graceful willows turned into thick woods beyond the water. A garden sat on a plot of flat land off to the side. It overflowed with plump tomatoes, lush heads of green lettuce, and beans. I couldn't imagine planting the Chou here—the gardener would discover it almost immediately.

Still, if Madame Faucon was to believe that I was

intent on gardening, I had to plant the Chou some-where in the vicinity. I skirted the garden and con-tinued down a winding walking path lined with graceful trees and lovely clumps of violets, betony, and pimpernels.

Around the first bend, I stepped off the path into a small patch of sunshine. According to *Advances in Plant Knowledge*, some scientists believed that sun-shine fed plants, causing them to grow. I couldn't even begin to imagine how that might work, but if there was any truth to it, I was willing to give it a try.

The land dipped down here, making a small hol-low protected from the wind. Perfect.

I fell to my knees, grabbed a nearby stick, and began digging in the rich, loamy soil. As soon as the hole was deep enough to accommodate the Chou's roots, I lowered it into the ground. The Chou shuddered and then sighed as it settled in, obviously relieved to be back in the earth. I gently packed soil in around it, taking care to make sure the ground was smooth and even, then watered the Chou with a small flask I'd brought along.

I set the flask beside me and sat back, my hopeful

gaze fixed on the plant. I don't know what I expected. For it to ripen immediately, I suppose. But the colors didn't change.

I let out a disappointed sigh and then laughed at myself. Gardening wasn't like painting, where you could stir together a couple of colors and instantly create something new.

The Chou would ripen soon enough. And I would be right here when it did.

As the afternoon wore on, I was tempted to take refuge in the shade, but instead I curled up on my side and whispered promises to my sister about how I wouldn't leave her. Not now, not ever. That was the thing about families—our roots would tangle around each other as we grew, ensuring that we'd always be there for each other.

A black woodpecker attacked a nearby tree.

My mind turned back to the Toussaints. Surely, the rabbits wouldn't have stopped delivering because of one tiny missing Chou.

Footsteps alerted me to someone's approach. I sat up and shifted my position to hide the Chou behind my back, preparing to make the case for how I'd been enjoying a bit of peace and quiet after the bustle of the city.

I needn't have worried. Elodie appeared, carrying a polished silver tray laden with tea, apples, and cheese.

I remembered my sharp words from earlier.

"That was kind of you," I said, hoping she'd take it as a peace offering.

"Just doing my job." She refused to meet my eyes as she placed the tray on the ground.

So much for my peace offering. I reached for the green apple—part of the Rosaceae family. A small bucket weighted down one end of the tray. It was filled with water. For the Chou, presumably.

I searched Elodie's face as I bit into the apple's tart flesh, but her gaze was unreadable.

"Thank you for the water." I raised my hand to cover the fact that I was speaking with food in my mouth.

Elodie nodded curtly and busied herself pouring my tea. Though Maman would never approve of fraternizing with staff, I wished again that I knew how to bridge the valley between us. If only I hadn't spoken so harshly earlier.

I finished my apple and drizzled the water around the Chou. It pooled on the ground and then soaked in, wetting the soil.

"Madame Faucon thinks you should return to the house with me to freshen up before dinner," Elodie said.

"I think Madame Faucon should go dig a hole," I said, trading the bucket for a wedge of hard cheese.

I'd spoken out of frustration, but I thought I saw a flash of laughter in Elodie's eyes. I couldn't resist continuing. "Or perhaps weed the garden."

Elodie's lips twitched.

Maman would have fits if she caught me talking like this, but now that I'd started, I didn't want to stop. "Or muck out the chicken coop."

"She could sit on the eggs," Elodie said. Her voice was perfectly serious as she added a sugar cube to my tea, but now the edges of her lips curled up slightly.

"She'd probably insist on organizing them first," I said.

Elodie snorted and tried to hide it behind a fake cough.

While I searched for a way to continue our banter,

she drew herself up and pulled a blank mask across her face. "Is there anything else, Miss?"

I was disappointed by her formal tone, but it wasn't fair of me to expect her to act like we were friends, particularly not after how terribly I'd treated her in the carriage. "I'm sorry," I said earnestly. "I was worried earlier, but I shouldn't have taken it out on you."

"You were right," Elodie said politely. "I spoke out of turn."

I dropped the rest of the cheese back on the tray. "I know you don't approve of what I'm doing, but please, try to understand—I need this."

"And I need my post," she said. "Don't you see that you've already put it in jeopardy?"

I'd been so focused on the Chou that I hadn't thought about her post at all.

She blinked back tears. "My maman is sick. If I lose this work, we lose our home."

A flush of shame heated my face. "Elodie, I . . . I didn't know. But I won't let anything happen to your post—I promise."

She scooped up the tray. "Will there be anything else?"

There was one more thing. I bit my lower lip. I

hated to involve her any more than she already was, but since she'd asked . . . "Can you sit with the Chou for a few minutes?"

A storm of emotions crossed her face.

"Never mind," I said, desperately wishing I could take the question back. "Please forget I said any-thing—it wasn't fair."

"It's only that Madame Faucon is expecting me right back."

I couldn't believe she was actually considering my request. "I won't be long," I explained hopefully. "I need a quick word with the gardener."

Her eyes opened wide. "You're going to tell Henri?"

"Of course not! But he won't think anything of me asking a few questions."

I'd always thought a Chou bonne's job was to keep the Chou safe and hydrated, help with the harvest, and prepare the baby's first meal, but now I wondered if there was some secret to making the Chou ripen. I wished I'd paid more attention to the Chou bonne at Maman's party, but I'd been distracted by the carrion plant someone had brought along. (Her supporters were always trying to outdo each other to attract attention.)

The plant had looked like a starfish but smelled of rotting meat. As hard as I tried, I hadn't been able to figure out what family it belonged to.

There was little-to-no chance I would find a Chou bonne in the area, at least not without raising some serious questions, so Henri would have to do.

"Fine," she said, looking over her shoulder as if she feared Madame Faucon might suddenly appear. "But hurry."

As I moved away, I thought I heard Elodie wish me luck. Maman always said there was no such thing, but I couldn't help think that her sudden willingness to help was a good bit of luck, indeed.

I found Henri on the other side of the cottage, trimming a row of already perfect hedges.

"Good day, Miss," he said, lowering his shears. He bowed, causing a patch of snow-white hair to flop over his stormy blue eyes.

"Hello, Henri," I said, attempting a friendly smile. Unlike Jean-André, Henri had never appreciated my interest in gardening. "How are you today?"

"Can I help you with something?"

I looked around, suddenly tongue-tied. A tall green stalk with wispy blades grew amid a nearby patch of grass. "I'm worried about that *Phalaris arundinacea*," I blurted out.

"Phala-what?"

"Reed canary grass." I pointed to the grass. "Left to its own devices, it could become quite invasive."

A muscle in his jaw twitched. "I'll take care of it," he said. "Was there anything else?"

"I was only, well, the grounds look so nice. And the vegetables in the garden are always so healthy."

It was true—his garden produced more than the one back home. And it wasn't only the quantity—the vegetables were bigger and tastier, too. I'd come planning to ask him for general gardening tips, but the reed canary grass had given me an idea. "I'm trying to grow some cabbage in the city, but it doesn't seem to be taking. Do you have any tips?"

Cabbage were part of the Brassicaceae family. Chou hadn't been classified as part of any kind of family at all on account of the lack of scientists in our country and the lack of Chou in others. (People outside of Montpeyroux apparently birth their children the same as animals.) But the Chou shared so many similarities with cabbage—the same root structure, the same shape, core, and ribs—even the leaves were similar in size, if not in color or texture.

Henri seemed to swell up before my eyes. "There's a reason your family has kept me on for more than forty years."

I waited expectantly.

"As to my cabbage, it's nothing that plenty of sunshine, water, and fertilizer can't explain."

Fertilizer! Why hadn't I thought of that?

"Thank you," I said, executing the world's fastest curtsey.

He bowed and returned to work.

I hurried across the lawn. According to what little I'd read in *Advances in Plant Knowledge* before Maman snatched it away, scientists used to believe that plants ate the soil to grow, but alchemist J. B. van Helmont recently planted a tree in a pot of soil and proved that while the tree grew, the soil hardly lost any weight. It hadn't made any mention of fertilizer, but Jean-André often mixed compost from the kitchen into the soil before planting, and Henri used compost and droppings from the horses, so there must be something to it.

I worked my way around the garden until I reached a pen behind the stables.

Trying to breathe only through my mouth, I used a shovel to fill a nearby pail. Once I'd moved a safe distance away, I gulped a deep breath of fresh air only to find it tainted by the bucket in my hand. I set my jaw. It was hard to imagine how something as awful as fertilizer could help plants grow healthy and strong, but it was worth a try.

Elodie jumped up when I returned. "Any luck?"

Her gaze fell on the bucket.

"Fertilizer," I said.

She wrinkled her nose. "Will it work?"

"I don't see how it could hurt."

She picked up the mostly full tray and returned to her polite but distanced voice. "I must get back to the house or Madame Faucon will start to wonder. You'll be along soon?"

"Please tell her I'll take my dinner in my room later."

"You're going to have to come in at some point. It's

not as if you can stay out here all night."

"I can't leave her alone," I said, stroking the Chou. My hand warmed as if it were already curled around my sister's tiny fist.

Elodie sighed. "I'll return before dinner and watch the Chou while you go in to eat."

I smiled shyly. "Thank you."

Her help was more than I expected—more than I deserved.

She studied me for a moment as if deciding whether or not to respond before dropping into a curtsey and disappearing up the path.

Seconds later, I realized I'd brought way more fertilizer than I needed. I dumped half the bucket around the Chou and then used my shoes to gently work it down into the soil, grateful that I was still in my traveling boots and not one of the many fashionable, but impractical, slippers Maman insisted I wear otherwise. "There," I said. "Now let's see if that doesn't set things right."

I stroked the Chou's soft leaves, hoping for some response, but the baby inside only breathed steadily in and out.

An acorn dropped from overhead. A moment later, the sound of sticks breaking and leaves crunching came from the woods behind the clearing. I scrambled for a long, sturdy stick. "Hello?"

There was no answer, but the noise stopped. Holding the stick out in front of me, I entered the woods, cursing at the dried grass and needles that crunched underfoot.

Several steps later, the hairs on the back of my neck stood up. I glanced over my shoulder and froze. The forest around me fell silent as blood pulsed in my ears. Then everything rushed back, overwhelming me with its clarity.

Dirt flew through the air as the skunk-rabbit dug up the Chou.

"Noooo!" I shrieked, raising my stick above my head and charging toward the thief. I couldn't lose my sister. Not now.

Chapter Nine: *Quincy*

I hopped off the back of the carriage the moment it stopped in front of an enormous home far out in the country. A comfy ledge packed with luggage had allowed me to rest during the trip. As my body had recovered, my courage renewed. Before long, I'd be back at the Warren, my reputation shining brighter than a star in the nighttime sky.

The girl exited the carriage, a Chou-shaped bundle in her arms. She chatted with a smaller but more weathered-looking woman. My ears perked up when the older woman revealed that several Chou hadn't been delivered last night. Chesney had said it would be business as usual, but Durrell's call for a strike had apparently stirred up trouble.

I couldn't worry about that now. The girl (whose name I'd finally learned was Fleurine) took off around the side of the house. I followed, taking care to remain far enough behind so as not to alert her to my presence.

She didn't so much as look back as she made her way around a garden and down a twisting path, stopping when she reached a little clearing.

She sank to her knees, set the Chou down, and used a stick to begin digging. With a little luck, she'd poke her eye out. I felt bad for wishing her ill, but she was the enemy. Because of her, I was the scourge of the Warren.[12] Even if I had the chance to begin the pre-ripening process for her, I wouldn't. This girl didn't deserve the Chou—she was nothing more than a thief.

As soon as she returned to the house, I'd make my move. The Chou and I would be back at the Warren before nightfall.

The girl finished patting the dirt down around the Chou.

Go on, I thought. *Off with you.*

---

12. *Don't bother denying it—every single rabbit in the Warren was in danger because of me.*

Instead of leaving, she curled up and started whispering plans for their life together, promises of the relationship they'd have.

What a bunch of rotten carrots!

I needed a diversion.

I'd passed a mud daubers' nest closer to the garden. It was risky, but if I could get it over here without upsetting the wasps inside, it could buy me enough time to dig up the Chou. (Any guilt I might have felt at causing the girl harm was more than outweighed by the fact that she'd brought all this on herself. Besides, the transport rabbits reported that humans had all sorts of magical healing potions they called medicine—she'd be fine.)

I slowly backed away from the clearing and retraced my paw prints, pausing when I came upon the nest. It rested on the ground, four hollow tubes molded out of mud.

I sucked in a deep breath. If I was going to save the Chou, if I was going to redeem myself, this was something I had to do.

Footsteps sounded in the garden. *Please, Great Maman Rabbit, let this work.*

I bent over and slowly, carefully, lifted the nest from the ground.

The footsteps moved toward the path.

Holding the nest out in front of me, I began hopping as smoothly as I could manage. My front legs trembled, but I couldn't risk pulling the nest closer to my chest. Not that such a short distance would stop the wasps from attacking, but I didn't want to make it any easier for them than I had to.

Wait a twitch. I stopped jumping. No wasps had come out. And I hadn't spotted any near the nest, either. Holes littered its surface.

I slammed the nest down on the ground, frustrated that I'd wasted so much time on an abandoned nest. Then I froze, hoping the noise didn't call anyone to investigate.

When no one came, I returned to the clearing. The second girl—Elodie—arrived at the same time. I'd overheard enough of their argument in the carriage to know she was a servant of some sort. A good deal of tension still filled the air between the two girls.

If only I were big enough to give them both a good thumping and grab the Chou. Since that wasn't an option, I was going to have to come up with another idea. While I sat thinking, an acorn fell from the canopy. It plunked on the ground and rolled to a stop at my feet. A squirrel stood up on a branch overhead and squawked, apparently upset by the loss.

An idea came to me as if gifted by Great Maman Rabbit herself. I hurried through the woods, taking care not to make any noise as I gathered my supplies.

I quietly assembled a pile of acorns and sticks under the treees near the Chou and gnawed on a long vine I found near the water. By the time I was done, I was close to overheating. I stuffed the vine in my pouch and made my way to the water's edge, where I sucked in long, cool gulps.

Feeling refreshed, I hurried back to my supplies and set to work building my fright-device, first stacking the sticks in a square and then filling the frame with acorns. With the vine looped securely around one bunch of the sticks, I made my way around the clearing, edging as close to the Chou as I dared. Elodie had gone, leaving Fleurine alone with the Chou. I sucked in a deep breath.

Here goes nothing.

I lobbed an acorn high in the air and gave the vine a mighty tug.

The acorn landed perfectly, near enough the Chou to draw Fleurine's attention. A twitch later, twigs scraped and dozens of acorns rolled away from my contraption.

"Hello?" Fleurine called, jumping to her feet.

She picked up a long stick and held it out like a weapon as she entered the woods.

Now! Go, go, go! I sprang toward the Chou and began pawing at the dirt. But I didn't get far before the fur on my back stood at attention, warning me of danger.

I looked up.

Fleurine stood staring at me from the edge of the woods, her mouth open.

My mind raced to gauge the chances of digging up the Chou and making an escape before she reached me. Not good. Not good at all.

Chapter Ten: *Fleurine*

"Shoo," I yelled, storming toward the skunk-rabbit with my stick still high in the air.

The rabbit bolted.

"That's right," I yelled with more bravery than I felt. "Go on, get out of here!"

I chased after it long enough to see that I'd frightened it off, but I knew better than to think it was gone for good. If it went for reinforcements, I'd be in real trouble.

I fell down on my knees next to the Chou and finished digging the hole Skunk had started. Gently but quickly, I lifted the plant from the ground, set it in the half-full bucket of fertilizer, and took off running.

I couldn't return to the city—there was nowhere

to plant the Chou. But I couldn't stay here, either. I needed a safe spot, somewhere the rabbit wouldn't look. For all Maman's resources, I couldn't think of a single place where we'd be welcomed without question.

As I burst from the woods and raced across the lawn, an idea began forming. I'd come across an abandoned shack in the woods while horseback riding one afternoon when I was younger. I'd wanted to explore, but my nursemaid said it wasn't safe. No one would think to search for me there—not even a rabbit.

I ducked into the forest behind the hedges on the far side of the cottage. Even with trees protecting me from the hot sun, there wasn't so much as a whisper of a breeze and sweat soon pooled in all sorts of uncomfortable places. I peeked down at the bucket. If anything, the leaves were more wilted than this morning. At least the Chou's scent was still sweet and milky.

A gray squirrel stopped to lecture me for interrupting its day.

"Stick an acorn in it," I mumbled.

Behind me, sticks and twigs crackled. I raced through the woods, ignoring the branches tearing at my skin and clothes, wondering how the rabbit had found me.

"Fleurine!" a voice shouted.

Elodie? I slowed.

"Fleurine, wait!" Elodie plowed toward me, breathing heavily. Her skirt was ripped and a trickle of blood flowed down her cheek.

"What are you doing here?" I asked.

"I might ask the same of you."

I resumed my brisk pace. "I have to leave."

"Whatever for?" Elodie hurried behind me. "Please, can you stop for a moment?"

"There's no time. The rabbit found me."

"The rabbit?"

"It wants the Chou back."

"I don't know exactly what you've gotten yourself into, but maybe returning the Chou isn't such a bad idea."

I whirled to face her. "How can you say that?"

She put her hands on her hips. "Is it really a coincidence that the delivery problems started today?"

Whatever was going on with the deliveries wasn't my fault. I smacked a branch out of my way. "This is my *sister*. I'm not giving her up. No matter what."

"You can't disappear into thin air," Elodie said, changing tactics. "Madame Faucon will have a fit. And your maman is already going to have my head when she hears about my part in this. Imagine if she discovers I allowed you to run off into the woods."

"I already told you, I'll take care of your post."

"Fleurine, please. Have some sense—you don't have food, or water, or anything you need to survive."

"I'm not giving up. Not now."

Elodie peered into the bucket. Her voice softened. "I haven't seen a Chou since Camilla."

"I've got to get it into the ground. Somewhere the rabbit can't find it. You can come along or go back, but either way, I have to keep moving." I skirted a large rock, half expecting Elodie to retreat.

She scrambled over the rock. "The only thing that will get me fired faster than coming with you is letting you go off on your own."

"Suit yourself." I hadn't wanted to pressure her, but truthfully, I was grateful to have her by my side. We made our way through the woods, walking for the better part of the afternoon without speaking. I was longing for the flask I'd left behind in my rush to escape when we stumbled across a creek. The cool water slid down my throat, refreshing my body as well as my spirit. We resumed walking.

"Do you have any idea where you're going?" Elodie asked, picking burrs from her skirt.

I told her about the shack.

"Are we getting close?"

"I'm not sure." I'd been on horseback when I'd seen it—there was no way to gauge how long it'd take on foot. But Mount Angora towered in the distance. I made out the rabbit's two enormous ears and the gentle curve of its head. Maman said that from the other side, the mountain looked like a wolf. I'd never traveled to Gatineau so I couldn't say for sure, but I was glad to have the twin peaks as a compass to guide me in the right general direction.

"What are you going to name it?" Elodie asked.

"Pardon?"

"The baby. Have you picked out a name?"

"Not yet." The thought hadn't occurred to me. "Maman will surely have an opinion."

"Surely," Elodie said flashing me a small smile.

"She's not that bad." I laughed, though of course Maman always had to be in charge of everything. We made our way down a small hill, taking care not to stumble on the loose rocks. "What's your maman like?"

Elodie sighed heavily. I thought she wasn't going to answer, but then she started talking.

"When I was little, she was the most wonderful maman a child could have. No matter how tired she was, no matter how long her day, she always had time for a snuggle or a song. I hardly remember her without a smile on her face."

"And now?"

"She got sick not long after we lost Papá. Hasn't left her bed since."

"How long has it been?"

"We lost him in the Great Fire."

That was four years ago—practically forever.

"That must be very hard on you."

"It's Camilla and the others I worry about. I try to fill Maman's shoes as best I'm able, but I'm not around much and—well, it's hard, that's all."

I had no idea the pressure Elodie was under. No wonder she wasn't interested in a friendship—she was too busy nursing a sick maman and supporting a family. And from her side of the garden, it probably looked as if my life was perfect.

As we walked, I thought about what it must have been like growing up with a loving, tender maman. A maman that hugged and snuggled and sang.

Not that Maman didn't love me—I knew she only wanted the very best for me. Still, I couldn't help but long for the type of maman Elodie described—one that cared as much for my heart as she did for my future.

When I was little, Maman occasionally sat me on her lap or spoiled me with a hug. Every great once in a while, she invited me to join her daily beauty rituals, but she liked to relax in silence as she soothed her supposedly puffy eyes (as far as I could tell, Maman hadn't had puffy eyes a day in her life) with bread soaked in rose water.

I didn't care much for sitting quietly, and those mother-daughter events inevitably ended with her calling for my nursemaid, irritated by my many questions. (How did rose water help with puffy eyes? Why roses and not tulips or lilacs or lavender?

How did they make the rose water, anyway?)

I stepped over a rotted log.

"What would you name the baby if you could?" Elodie asked.

I had no idea where to begin. We passed a small patch of bushes blooming with tiny yellow flowers. "Garance?"

"Garance?"

I showed Elodie the flowers. "Pretty," she said.

They were, but I didn't like the shape the word *garance* made in my mouth. It was too harsh for a baby, for my sister. I wanted something softer. I spotted a cluster of reine-des-prés. "Or maybe Reine?"

"How about Rue?" Elodie asked.

Reine and Rue were better, but they still weren't quite right. *Sophie, Aubrey, Naomi—*

"I've got it!"

"Let me guess, another flower?"

"Not a flower. Aimée."

"Aimée?"

I switched the bucket from my right hand to my left. The welt where the handle had dug into my palm pulsed.

"It means *beloved*." I liked how the word flowed over my tongue. The shape was soft—sweet.

"It's pretty," Elodie said. "But what if it's a boy?"

I swatted a cobweb from my face. "It's not."

"How do you know?"

"I just do." This Chou carried a girl, the little sister I'd always dreamed of.

"What if you're wrong?"

I was saved from having to answer by the sight of a hollowed cedar tree twisting into the air in front of us. "This is it! This is the place!"

I rushed ahead, eager to replant the Chou. To meet my sister. *Aimée*.

A small structure squatted in a meadow beyond the cedar. A gentle stream trickled in the distance. As we approached, my stomach squeezed tight. The shack was in worse shape than I remembered. Half a wall was collapsed, and the ceiling looked as though it might cave in any moment.

"This is . . . where we're supposed to stay?" Elodie asked.

"It's not exactly like I remember it. But it'll have to do. There isn't any place else."

Elodie followed me around the shack.

A small clearing bathed in the late afternoon sun.

"This'll be the perfect spot for the Chou." I ripped out fistfuls of dried grass until I reached the bare ground. Then I grabbed a nearby stick and began loosening the dirt.

Elodie kneeled to join me. When the hole was ready, I checked over my shoulder to make sure the rabbit hadn't followed us. I stabbed my stick into the ground. If only Skunk had left well enough alone, the poor Chou wouldn't have to endure yet another transplant. *If Skunk had left well enough alone, you wouldn't have the Chou in the first place.* I brushed the thought aside—the last thing the thieving rabbit deserved was my gratitude.

Sweat trickled down my back. For the third time that day, I carefully placed the Chou in the ground. Again, it seemed as though the Chou gave a sigh of relief. Elodie and I scooped dirt around the roots, taking care to mix in the fertilizer.

I frowned and bent closer. The edges of the leaves were browning.

"Is something wrong?" Elodie asked.

I couldn't bring myself to share my concern.

"It's fine," I said, willing my words to be true. Chou were hearty—they had to be in order to survive transport in a rabbit's pouch.

Elodie excused herself to freshen up at the creek and inspect the shack.

Crickets chirped. I stroked the Chou's soft leaves. "I can't wait to meet you."

Aimée squirmed gently. Warmth entered through my fingertips and flowed up my arm as if we were connected by a magical thread.

As I used the now-empty bucket to fetch water, my hope soared like a marsh tern riding the wind. The Chou would surely start to ripen overnight.

My stomach rumbled as I settled back at the Chou's side and moistened the dirt. The light was nearly gone; foraging would have to wait until morning.

Elodie called from the front of the shack. "It might be safe to sleep in."

"I'm sleeping out here."

"It's far too dangerous," Elodie said, rounding the corner and striding toward me.

"If it's too dangerous for me, then it's too dangerous for the Chou." I folded my arms.

Elodie cocked her head. "You really think your maman is going to be okay with any of this?"

I picked up the stick I'd used to dig earlier and began drawing random designs in the dirt. The activity reminded me of my first nursemaid. Frustrated with my lack of progress learning letters, she'd taken me out to the garden and had me practice drawing them with my fingers in the soil.

The practice had planted the letters firmly in my brain, but Maman dismissed the maid the moment she found out. By then it was too late—I'd already fallen in love with the feel of dirt under my nails, with the smell of damp earth in my nose. With the fresh air, the freedom—the possibility. I had a string of nursemaids after that, none of them able to live up to Maman's impossible expectations. "She will be," I said. "Besides, what's she going to do—send the baby back?"

Give her to the Toussaints, a voice whispered in my head. I scooted closer to the Chou. I wouldn't let anyone take my sister away.

By now, the sun had sunk below the horizon, and

the sky had darkened to the bluish black of a fresh bruise.

I bent over the Chou, searching again for signs of ripening.

Disappointed, I straightened and rubbed my aching back. Every part of my body protested all of the unusual activity it'd been forced to endure recently. Sleeping on the ground for a second night wasn't going to help. But by this time tomorrow, I'd be back at the cottage, my little sister in my arms.

Out of the corner of my eye, I saw Elodie reach for a patch of weeds growing from the base of the shack.

"Elodie, stop!"

But it was too late. Her head snapped up as her hand closed around a bunch of bright green leaves.

She gasped and let go.

"Ouch!" she cried, cradling her sore hand to her chest. "What in the warren is that?"

"Stinging nettle. Let's get you to the creek."

I hovered over her, watching for an allergic reaction as she plunged her injured hand into the cool water.

After soaking it, she pulled her hand from the

water and shook it out, sending droplets flying through the air.

I wiped one from my cheek.

"That was like a hundred bee stings all at once," she said.

She didn't show any signs of breathing difficulties or stomach upset. "Is the pain gone?"

"No, but it's better. Thank you."

She examined her palm as we walked back to the shack.

"What were you doing, anyway?" I asked.

"I thought if we cleared this little area, we could sleep up alongside the wall. That way, we'd be close to the Chou but not quite so out in the open."

"Thank you," I said. "It was a good thought, but we can't risk getting stung again."

We settled down on either side of the Chou. I gazed up at the stars and picked out the Rabbit's Ears. I tried to find the Carrot, too, but it was the wrong time of year.

Next to me, Elodie began singing. I'd never heard anything so lovely. Her voice filled the darkness with a sound as soft and velvety as the Chou's leaves.

The song she sang was familiar—a lullaby from my childhood.

Sweet Chou, delivered in the dark
Took my sad life and made it sweeter
Your joy, your laughter, even your tears
Made it all the sweeter

When I was little, I used to hold a small doll Maman had someone make for me—a soft baby with Chou leaves sprouting from her back. I wrapped the leaves around her and sang this song over and over until I fell asleep, hoping that when I woke up, it'd be a real little sister in my arms. That was back when I still clung to the hope that Maman might set out a bundle of purple carrots, when I was sure that she'd one day agree to add a sister to our family.

My stomach pinched as I thought about telling Maman that I'd gone behind her back, but I swept my nerves aside.

A true leader never wavers, Maman always said. She might be upset at first, but she'd be proud of the initiative I'd taken, of the problems I'd solved to make this happen.

By now, Elodie had switched to a new song, one that spoke of heartache and heartbreak, of longing and love. Her voice rivaled the very best at the opera. With the proper training, there'd be no end to what she could achieve. But she'd said she needed this job to support her family. She could no more hope for voice training than I could hope to avoid attending Maman's Académie of Leadership.

The warm night air was suddenly oppressive. I leaned over the Chou, hoping to inspect the leaves for a change in color. But the stars that had shined so brightly earlier in the evening were almost completely gone, no doubt obscured by the clouds I vaguely remembered seeing off in the distance earlier in the day. I sighed and curled up in a ball. Elodie kept singing. My eyelids slipped lower, lower, lower. . . .

Chapter Eleven: *Quincy*

I blundered through the woods, not knowing where I was going, seeking only to escape Fleurine's fury. Eventually, I realized that she'd gone back to the Chou. I stopped, desperate to catch my breath and regulate my temperature. Once I cooled down, my good sense kicked in. I had to try again. If nothing else, I could go back to my original idea to wait until she went in for the night and snatch the Chou then.

At least that was my plan.

It would have been a good one if my cabbage-brained brother hadn't shown up. That's right—Durrell. He sprang out from behind a tree and landed directly in my path.

"Durrell! What are you doing here? How did you find me?" My ears lay back against my head.

"Good afternoon, greetings, good day to you, too," he said, pressing his forehead against mine.

"Good afternoon, greetings, good day," I muttered, pulling back. The last thing I needed was him jumping in and taking over.

He binkied. "Am I ever glad to see you! When the river swept you away, I thought you were a goner for sure. I combed the banks downstream, trying to pick up your scent."

My nose twitched. Since when did Durrell care what happened to me?

He continued. "Luckily, I met up with Dion."

(Dion is another transport rabbit—he and Durrell are practically inseparable when they aren't out making deliveries.)

"He saw you on the back of a carriage belonging to the Grande Lumière when he was out searching. It didn't take a full basket of carrots to figure out where to find you. Now come on, let's get you back to the Warren."

I rested on my haunches, trying to look cool and

collected and hoping he couldn't hear my heart thumping. "I'm not going anywhere."

Durrell's ears swiveled impatiently. "I've got a Chou to find. The sooner I get you back, the sooner I can get to work."

Of course. He wanted to get me out of the way so he could find the Chou and return a hero. As usual. I hopped backward. "I'm not going back to the Warren."

"Quincy, it's not safe for you out here."

"Says you. I've been doing fine on my own."

"Really? Because last time I checked, you nearly drowned. What are you doing out here, anyway? You know only transport rabbits are allowed to leave the Warren."

"None of your business."

"None of my business?" He hopped closer. "Do you know what I was *supposed* to be doing last night?"

I hung my head.

"Delivering Chou. You want to know what I was doing instead?" His back foot thumped angrily. "Searching for you and the missing Chou. And I'm not the only one. The Committee pulled a bunch of us from transport."

That explained the undelivered Chou. But I was in no mood for Durrell's lecture. "What do you care about being pulled from transport? I thought you wanted to go on strike anyway."

"That doesn't mean I—"

But I wasn't finished. "Maybe I'm out looking for the Chou, too, did you ever think of that? Did it ever occur to you that you don't have to be the hero all the time, that the rest of us are worth something?"

Durrell pulled back. "What does being a hero have anything to do with—"

Something cracked in the woods behind us. Durrell and I both swiveled our ears, gauging the danger. Branches broke as something—or someone—moved toward us.

A hulking brown bear emerged from the brush.

"Run!" Durrell yelled.

His word echoed in my head, but my brain couldn't make sense of it.

The bear opened its mouth and let out a rumbling roar. It lifted an enormous paw, revealing long, sharp claws.

Run, run, run. . . . The word bounced around in my

head. This time, my brain recognized it, but my body refused to move.

The bear's paw sliced through the air, aiming directly for the top of my skull.

I squeezed my eyes shut and braced for the deadly blow.

Something knocked me sideways, sending me spinning head over paws and breaking my trance.

The bear bellowed, filling the forest with its rage.

"This way," Durrell yelled, untangling our limbs and zigzagging through a patch of low brush.

Without thinking, I followed.

We burst out the other side and continued hopping. It took several minutes to realize the bear hadn't given chase. A shallow creek trickled ahead. Durrell and I plunged ourselves into the cool water, desperate to lower our body temperatures. Our mouths hung open as we panted.

Red water streamed from Durrell's golden fur.

"You're hurt!"

"It's nothing."

"Let me see."

He turned and I inspected the deep gash across his

shoulder. My stomach quivered at the sight of his raw flesh. Then I remembered being hit from the side—being flung out of the way of the bear's paw. Durrell.

Durrell, who I would have sworn lived to torment me. Durrell, who'd spent the entire day searching for me. Durrell, who had risked his life to save mine. The truth hit me like the moon falling from the sky. I'd always thought love was warm and soft and fuzzy, like a newborn kitten.[13] Durrell's love didn't look anything like that, but it was there all the same.

Shame washed through me, raising my body temperature all over again. "It's not nothing. We have to get you back to the Warren before it's too late." (Not even the Warren's magic can restore life once it's been lost.)

He groaned. "The Chou . . ."

"The Chou can wait!"

"It can't, and you know it. Even if the Chou survives, the strike is going to start tomorrow at dusk."

"I'm not leaving you."

---

13. *Baby rabbits are called kittens, too, you know.*

"I can make it back to the Warren," he insisted. "You have to continue the search."

His gaze held mine as he waited for a promise I didn't want to make. But he was right. That Chou contained a baby. A life. Of all the animals in the world, Great Maman Rabbit had created us to grow and deliver them. To keep them safe. We'd never lost one, and we couldn't start now. Blood continued to flow from Durrell's wound.

"Fine," I said. "But we have to get you to a tunnel first."

Although there wasn't enough magic in the tunnels to heal him, there was almost certainly enough to keep him alive until he made it back to the Warren. Durrell whimpered and groaned as we made our way through the woods. Finally, we reached a shrub-covered entrance.

"You sure you're going to be all right?" I asked, half hoping he'd change his mind and ask me to accompany him.

His whiskers twitched. "I could still take you down."

We both knew it wasn't true.

I rested my forehead against his. "May the Great

Maman Rabbit guide you," I whispered.

"You too, cabbage-breath. Now get moving."

Shadows that seemed cool and soothing in the heat of the day turned long and threatening as I made my way back to the Chou.

I pressed on, relieved my brother had made it to the relative safety of the tunnel but struggling to make sense of his warning about the strike. Trying to grow more purple carrots was one thing. But we were already starving, and a strike would only make matters worse. The Committee had to know that. Plus, they were always going on about honor and duty and the importance of our work.

Maybe they felt backed into their burrows and believed this was the only way to save us. Or maybe they hadn't agreed to the strike—maybe the transport rabbits were planning it on their own. Either way, I had to get that Chou back.

The woods began to thin, and I caught a glimpse of a familiar house through the trees.

I approached the clearing where the Chou was planted, stopped behind an elderberry bush, and rose up on my hind legs, sniffing. Unless I was mistaken, there weren't any humans nearby. This was my chance!

I sprang into the open. An empty hole greeted me.

A crow heckled me from overhead. *Worthless. Worthless. Worthless.*

I was tempted to flop down on the ground, to let the owls or whatever else was prowling the woods have me. But Durrell believed in me. He would never give up. I couldn't either.

The Chou's sweet, milky scent still lingered in the air, but it was tinged slightly sour. Time was running out. I perked up my ears, listening carefully for Fleurine's footsteps. There were only the sounds of leaves whispering, squirrels chattering, and staff murmuring near the house.

Stupid ears. If they were as big as a Committee member's—or even a regular size—I'd be able to track her with no problem.

I lowered my nose to the ground and detected the faintest hint of onion and lavender. I followed the scent trail out of the meadow, up the path, across the lawn, and into the woods. A new smell mixed in—not lavender but distinctly female. Elodie. With the traces both of them left behind, I'd have no trouble finding their new spot.

Apparently, some of Durrell's confidence had seeped into me, because I didn't slow as I entered the thick canopy of trees that cut off what little light remained.

I had no idea how far I'd gone before the air changed. The wind picked up and the temperature dropped. A storm was coming quickly. I sniffed but found no sign that the girls—or the Chou—were in my immediate vicinity.[14] What were they doing all the way out here, anyway? From what I'd heard of humans, they stuck close to their shelters at night.

Then again, so did rabbits. I lowered my nose and continued on. Several twitches later, light mist sprayed down on my fur.

Uh-oh. If the rain arrived before I found the girls, I'd lose their scent. No sooner had the thought crossed my mind than a fat drop plopped on my nose. And then another. I rushed through the woods, cursing my luck.

---

14. *In other words, they're nowhere around.*

The rain became harsher, more insistent. It rolled off the fur on my back, but the drops pelted my face. Wind gusted and howled.

Lightning flashed, followed by a loud clap of thunder. My fur stood up, warning me to take cover.

I dashed toward a patch of dense greenery that hid a swollen creek. Lightning flashed again.

CRACK!

An opening to a burrow peeked from behind a clump of tall grass. I sniffed the entrance and detected the lingering scent of a former resident—a badger, if I wasn't mistaken.

CRACK!

I dove inside the hole as the rain turned to hail.

Something squeaked. I sniffed again. Mice. They were harmless enough, but something must have chased them from their home or they would never have taken cover in a space this large.

I pushed my way deeper inside. The squeaking intensified. Another streak of lightning revealed a maman standing tall in front of a nest filled with babies. She was obviously chewing me out, but I wasn't going anywhere, not in this weather. I crouched, muscles tense, as the storm grew in intensity.

I hoped it would blow over soon, but even after the hail passed, pounding rain made it clear that I had a long night ahead of me.

My nose twitched with worry and my stomach resumed its earlier cramping. I longed for the comfort of my burrow, for the mass of my siblings' warm bodies, for Maman. As envious as I'd been of the transport rabbits, it had never occurred to me how much they risked each and every time they left the Warren.

It wasn't fair, the dangers we endured for a few puny carrots. Back when the Angora Rex were alive, they never went hungry. No one knew what had supposedly caused the plague that destroyed the giant carrots and the Rex along with them, but I'd seen enough of the human world to know that they must've had something to do with it.

And now the girl had found the Warren. If word got out, it was a safe bet that the greedy humans would try to take over and upset the natural balance orchestrated by Great Maman Rabbit herself.[15]

---

15. *Whatever your feelings about Great Maman Rabbit, you must admit that this world is far too extraordinary to have been created entirely by chance.*

Outside, the storm raged.

There was no chance of returning the Chou tonight. At this rate, it seemed unlikely that I'd be able to find it tomorrow, either. I scratched an angry itch behind my ear. Bringing the Chou back wouldn't be enough anyway—not if the girl exposed us.

Thoughts of humans overrunning the Warren plagued me. Every time I fought them off, they were replaced by thoughts of the strike. I remembered how upset the woman back at the house had been when only a few Chou weren't delivered. I couldn't imagine what the humans would do when we stopped delivering Chou altogether, but it wouldn't be anything good. (We're talking about people who once started a war over a stolen cooking pot.)

If we weren't careful, we were going to end up like the Angora Rex—only no one would be putting up statues of us when we were gone.

I was trying to distract myself with a bath when tiny bodies rustled in the nest. Maman Mouse's loud squeak filled the cavern. A warm body rubbed up against my side, then another. Soon, five mice cuddled in my fur. I sat frozen in place, wondering what to do.

Maman said mice were nothing but a nuisance. Durrell would urge me to chase them away.

But Maman and Durrell weren't here. And these pups were undoubtedly cold and frightened. I thought about little Sophie, wondered who she was spending the night snuggled with.

"We'll ride out the storm together," I murmured.

Maman Mouse squeaked.

"I'm not any happier about it than you are."

But I relaxed and settled in, secretly glad for the company.

Chapter Twelve: *Fleurine*

I startled awake, sensing something was wrong. Tears rolled down my cheeks. No, not tears. Water. Rain. More of a mist, really, but the air was thick and heavy. Threatening.

"Elodie," I whispered, nudging her. "Elodie, wake up."

She groaned and rolled over. I shook her shoulder. "Elodie, it's raining. We have to move inside."

She pushed herself to sitting and wiped her face, then groaned. "All right," she said, climbing to her feet. "Let's go."

Though clouds covered the moon, the faint outline of the Chou was reassuring. I hated to leave my sister, but the Chou's waterproof leaves could handle the rain better than Elodie or I. We stumbled around to the front of the cabin. The door creaked as we pushed inside. Something small scuffled in the dark.

"Hello," I called. I knew it was silly—if someone were here, Elodie would have found out earlier. But the silence comforted me enough to continue. Although the back wall was partially collapsed, the front seemed sound. Elodie and I edged toward a corner. I brushed a sticky cobweb from my face. We sank down on the floor, shivering in our damp clothes.

"At least we're not drenched," Elodie said.

Lightning illuminated the room, exposing the severed head of a wooden doll on the floor. Thunder rattled the walls. Rain began pouring down, beating against the roof. My thoughts turned back to the Chou. As if reading my mind, Elodie comforted me. "The Chou will be fine."

That didn't mean Aimée wasn't scared. "Maybe I should check."

Elodie rested a hand on my arm. "It won't do the Chou any good for you to catch a cold."

I settled back down, wishing we had a blanket to wrap around our shoulders.

The rain continued. A drip began over our heads. We scooted farther into the corner. Another bolt of lightning exposed a rickety, overturned chair. Thunder boomed almost simultaneously.

"That was close," I said.

"We'll be safe in here," Elodie assured me.

The rain turned to hail. I sprang to my feet.

"What are you—" The end of Elodie's sentence was drowned out as I wrenched the door open, shot around the side of the building, and flung myself over the Chou, cradling it protectively under my stomach. Hard, pea-sized pellets beat down on me, stinging my back. I squeezed my eyes shut.

Then someone was beside me, pushing me away. I refused to move. Elodie shoved the upside-down bucket in my face. Finally, I understood—she was trying to help. I rose as she slid it over the top of the Chou. Suddenly, the hair on my arms stood up and the air crackled. An arc of lightning stretched from the black sky straight down to the roof of the shack.

CRACK!

I screamed and stumbled backward.

A flame shot up from the spot where the lightning

hit, but it was immediately extinguished by the hail. The already unstable shack shuddered, and then the roof collapsed, followed by the walls.

Elodie and I ran for the woods, our arms raised to protect our faces from the icy pellets that continued pummeling us.

A cluster of small trees provided some shelter. Pounding rain replaced the hail. We clung to each other, drenched and shivering.

An eternity passed before the rain slowed to a drizzle and then stopped altogether. We pulled apart.

"Are you all right?" I asked, wringing out my wet hair and rubbing the back of my neck, which stung from what felt like a million arrows.

"I'm fine. You?"

"I wouldn't mind a good fire."

"You very nearly had one," Elodie said, wrapping her arms around herself and nodding toward the shack, which was nothing more than a heap of broken boards.

I shivered as I hurried toward the Chou. "We could have been in there."

"The Grande Maman in the Moon was looking out for us," Elodie said.

Hopefully the Grande Maman had been watching out for the Chou, too. The clouds had passed, and the bucket glinted in the moonlight. I lifted it up. The Chou seemed to have weathered the storm without any damage.

Relieved, I sank down in the wet grass.

Elodie settled next to me. "Are you ever going to tell me about the rabbit?"

"Now?"

"Unless you have something better to do."

I wanted to sleep, but I was shivering too hard for that to happen.

Elodie cleared her throat, letting me know that she was waiting. I wondered how much to tell her. If I wanted a real friendship, it had to be everything.

I filled her in, pausing to answer her questions as I went.

"I can't believe you actually found the Warren," she murmured when I finally finished.

The Warren. It still hardly seemed possible. Everything had happened so fast that the memories felt like a dream. But the Chou in front of me proved otherwise.

And now it was my responsibility. This wasn't like my plantings back home—the Chou contained a living, breathing person.

A mosquito bit my neck.

I groaned. "This might be the longest night of my life."

"If this is the worst you've ever had it," Elodie said, "then you're doing fine."

I didn't want to pry, but I was curious. "Want to talk about it?"

I felt her shrug. "After Papá died, supporting the family fell to me. I found work where I could, but nothing steady. Before getting this post, there were plenty of times where we didn't have enough fuel for heat, or light, or even enough food."

I tried to imagine making it through a winter night without a fireplace blazing. Or going to bed with an empty stomach night after night. Or supporting an entire family.

"What about care baskets?"

"What about them?"

"They should have helped." Maman had started the program several years earlier. Funded by the city, baskets filled with food and other essentials were delivered to anyone in need.

"They did, at first. But then I turned twelve and we weren't eligible."

"What do you mean?"

"The care baskets aren't available if there's anyone in the home who can work."

"But you were only twelve!"

Elodie bumped me as she shifted. "Plenty old enough for a job."

I sat rooted by horror.

In all the times Maman bragged about the care program, she never mentioned this part of it. She must not know—she couldn't possibly. I'd have to bring it to her attention as soon as we returned. "I'm sorry."

"Doesn't matter," Elodie said. "I was lucky to land this post."

No wonder she'd agreed to travel to the cottage with no notice. She'd said that her maman was sick, but I hadn't really understood. I tried to imagine getting a job. "How did you get this position?"

"Bernadette is my aunt. She put in a good word for me."

I couldn't stop thinking about what might have happened to Elodie and her sisters if her aunt wasn't our cook. Someone's ability to support their family shouldn't depend on who they knew. Then again, my entire life depended on who I knew—who I was related to. Being born a d'Aubigné guaranteed I'd never have to worry about a thing. Or at least not about things like starving or losing my home.

My head began to ache. It was too much for me to think about—I didn't know how Elodie managed. The only thing I knew for sure was that she wasn't going to lose her post over a mess I'd dragged her into—not if I could help it.

Elodie hummed, wrapping me in the comfort of a sweet lullaby. I didn't think sleep would come anytime soon, but it wasn't long before I curled up on the ground and slipped into the dark of my dreams.

Someone stirred next to me. Birds chirped overhead. I pried my eyes open. Bright sunlight highlighted Elodie's mud-streaked face. I sat up and brushed an ant from my arm. The collapsed shack taunted me with memories of the previous night. I spun to check on the Chou. It hadn't ripened at all. Worse, the edges of the leaves were even more wilted. "Do you smell that?" I asked.

"What?" Elodie asked.

The Chou's sweet scent carried a hint of sour.

I rested a hand on the leaves, feeling for signs of breathing. "She's alive," I whispered.

Elodie sat up and rubbed her eyes. "The storm was a lot for her to handle, but she'll recover."

"Do you think so?"

"We'll know soon enough."

If Aimée was hurt, I'd never forgive myself. But Elodie was right—if the Chou didn't ripen through-out the day, I'd know for sure something was wrong. I decided to give it until high noon. If there were no signs of improvement, we'd have to return to the cottage. Madame Faucon could help us procure the services of a Chou bonne.

"Why don't you wash up?" Elodie said.

Squatting at the edge of the creek, I splashed cool water over my face and attempted to rinse the edges of my filthy skirt. It was no use—after a night on the muddy ground, the whole thing was a mess. I wrung it out and cringed. Maman would faint if she could see me.

I waded across the creek to inspect some promising bushes. My heart quickened as I noted the maple-shaped leaves and gently striated green fruit. Gooseberries! They were part of the Grossulariaceae family and, more importantly, edible.

After testing the fruit's firmness to make sure it was sufficiently ripe, I gathered as many as I could in my skirt (taking care to avoid the thorns) and hauled them back to Elodie. "Breakfast," I called.

She was still sprawled next to the Chou. "Thank goodness. I'm starving."

We stuffed handfuls of tart berries into our mouths without any regard for proper manners. Sticky juice ran down our fingers, and we licked them clean. The rain had cleared some of the moisture from the air, making the hot weather more bearable. I checked on the Chou.

It hadn't changed a bit. I fretted. What was it Maman always said? *A watched pot never boils.* I snorted. More like a watched Chou never ripens.

But this one would. And then we'd return to the cottage, all three of us. I imagined Madame Faucon's face when I showed her my little sister. She'd demand we clean up straight away, but first I'd have to figure out how to turn the Chou's leaves into a bottle of Lait de Chou. (Without these essential nutrients, she wouldn't survive on the diluted goat's milk she would drink until starting on solids.)

"Do you think we should return to the city tonight or wait until first light?"

"First light. We still have a long walk back."

She was right. But I didn't know if I could wait until tomorrow to introduce Aimée to Maman. She was visiting Rion, at least a day away by carriage, but for an emergency like the rabbits not delivering, she'd probably ridden horseback, cutting her travel time back to Mignon in half. For the briefest of moments, I felt badly for springing another daughter on her in the midst of the problems with the protestors and the rabbits. *But this isn't another problem—it's a gift*, I reminded myself.

Elodie slept most of the morning. I was exhausted, but I couldn't stop checking on the Chou. I passed the time by turning the ring on my finger again and again and jumping at every noise in the woods. By the time high noon arrived, my stomach felt as though it was filled with heavy stones. The baby's breath was steady, but the Chou wasn't improving, much less ripening. Save an occasional squirm here or there, Aimée hardly showed any signs of activity. *What if she's unwell?* The thought wrapped itself around my brain like an unwelcome weed.

Finally, I woke Elodie. "We have to return to the cottage."

"You know what that will mean?" she asked.

My gaze fell on the old, gnarled cedar that had long since given up on life. Tears burned my eyes. Asking for help was a huge risk, but I'd never forgive myself if something happened to my sister.

"There's no choice."

Elodie switched to the brisk efficiency I was used to. "Very well," she said. "We have a long walk ahead of us. You'd better gather berries again— we're not going to make it without more food in our bellies."

This time I could hardly stomach the fruit's sour taste. I couldn't let myself think about what might happen when we returned. For now, I had to focus on the journey ahead of us, on getting back to the cottage as quickly as possible.

After washing up, I kneeled in front of the Chou. "This is the last time, I promise."

With trembling hands, I dug it up and nestled it into the bucket with dirt around the roots.

"Let's go," I said.

A vulture circled high overhead.

Where I'd crashed through the woods yesterday, today I forced myself to move with calmness, with intention. It was only by focusing on the mechanics of placing one foot in front of the other that I could bear the sharp pain threatening to rip open my chest.

Madame Faucon would try to whisk my sister off and put her in the care of a Chou bonne. If I let her out of my sight, there would be no guarantee that I'd ever get her back. The thought made it feel as if my lungs were breaking right along with my heart.

Elodie led the way, stopping occasionally to hold particularly large branches so that they didn't spring back and hit me in the face. I stumbled over a shrub and landed wrong on my foot, twisting my ankle. The sharp pain made my leg buckle. My grip on the bucket's handle slipped.

Time stood still as I imagined the Chou spilling out and crashing to the ground. I regained my balance and lunged for the handle. My fist closed around it. The bucket dangled in the air, inches from the ground.

"Are you all right?" Elodie asked.

I tested my ankle. It ached, but after the initial shock, most of the pain passed. We set off again with me fretting over how close I'd come to dropping the Chou. I was still berating myself when Elodie guided us to the bank of the creek that gurgled nearby. We refreshed ourselves by gulping the cool, clear water and splashing it on our faces. I wetted the Chou's roots.

Elodie sank down on a rock covered in soft green moss.

"What are you doing?" I asked. "We have to keep moving."

"I need to rest." She tugged off her boots. Swollen blisters covered both heels.

I cringed. "That must hurt."

She grimaced as she plunged her feet in the creek.

I set the Chou down on the bank. "We'll get you fixed up as soon as we're back."

"Why don't you go on without me?" Elodie said. "We're nearly there and I can make my way back on my own."

"I'm not leaving you here." Over the course of the night, something had shifted between us. Elodie didn't feel like staff anymore—she felt like a friend. I wondered if the woods always had that effect on people. Maybe it was the fresh air that had caused us to open up. Or the fact that we'd been forced to rely on each other. Or maybe it was our fear that had bonded us. One thing was clear: out here, our differences weren't so important.

"You have the Chou to think about."

"I also have you to think about," I said. "Now that's enough of that."

Still, I twisted and fidgeted and finally reached over to a cluster of tempest's lace. The feathery greens were identical to carrot greens, but the delicate blossoms on top were orange and larger than the white ones on the carrots Jean-André grew in the garden. (I'd never left my purple carrots in the ground long enough to know what their blooms might look like.)

I brought the cluster to my nose. The sweet smell reminded me of the time I'd gathered a bouquet for Maman and rushed in the house to offer up my gift; she'd been in an important meeting with one of her conseillères and scolded me for interrupting.

I mindlessly ran my fingers over the blossoms, gently tugging them from their stems. A handful of seeds fell into my hand along with the petals.

I gasped.

"What is it?" Elodie said.

"It's only—these seeds are shiny and purple!"

"So what?"

"So they look exactly like purple carrot seeds! If I saw the two side by side, I doubt I'd be able to tell a difference."

She wasn't the slightest bit interested in my discovery, but my mind raced. Tempest's lace was thought to be part of the Brassicaceae family along with kale and broccoli, but what if it was actually a part of the Apiaceae family?

I yanked the entire plant out of the ground,

angering a bee hovering over a blossom. The root was bulbous and white—an awful lot like the deformed purple carrots I'd grown. Was it coincidence that the purple carrot seeds had started producing something so similar to tempest's lace? What if somehow the seeds had mixed together to make a new kind of plant—something that wasn't fully a purple carrot but that was no longer tempest's lace, either?

I remembered the chapter in *Advances in Plant Knowledge* that had suggested plants may reproduce by moving pollen around their blooms. If that was true, maybe it was possible that a purple carrot and a tempest's lace plant had somehow rubbed together, mixing up their pollens.

I began pacing, certain that I was still missing something. My theory explained our problems growing purple carrots, but it didn't explain why the rabbits wouldn't have accepted the bunches of partially purple carrots I left for them—were they really that picky?

"You ready?" Elodie asked.

I wanted to inspect the tempest's lace and its seeds more closely, but we had to keep moving.

Elodie winced as she put her boots back on.

I gathered a handful of soft green mullein leaves from a nearby plant. "Here," I said, handing them over. "Tuck these in your shoes. It won't take away the pain, but it'll help the rubbing."

"I'm not sure they'll fit," Elodie said.

She stuffed the leaves into her already-too-small shoes. I pursed my lips. Another thing I'd be talking to Maman about when this was all over.

Elodie winced as we set off, and there was definitely a limp in her step. She broke out in song, undoubtedly an attempt to take her mind off her pain. This time, it was a lively jingle I didn't recognize. Her voice was warm and inviting, and I soon found myself humming along as my purple carrot theory looped over and over in my mind.

Suddenly, Elodie came to a stop in front of me. She quit singing and held up her hand, motioning for silence as she addressed someone I couldn't yet see. "Good day."

"Good day," a boy's familiar voice answered.

I peeked around her and gasped. "Ignace! What are you doing out here?"

He was dressed the same as yesterday, minus the straw hat. A tangle of thick auburn curls framed his face.

"I might ask you the same thing."

"We're . . . out for a walk," I said, hiding the bucket behind my back.

"You two know each other?" Elodie asked.

Ignace's gaze followed the bucket. "I had the pleasure of making her acquaintance yesterday. I happened to be passing by your estate this morning when I got flagged down and recruited to help search."

So much for hoping he wouldn't figure out who I was. But that was the least of my worries. I cringed thinking of the chaos I'd caused back at the cottage. Madame Faucon must be beside herself. And Maman—she had to be aware of my absence by now. I couldn't even imagine what she must be going through.

He raised his eyebrows. "Apparently, you went missing again. Everybody has been ordered to join the search." He folded his arms. "Even those of us with better things to do."

"I'm perfectly fine," I said, bristling at the irritated

tone in his voice. "And anyway, I'm on my way back."

Elodie cleared her throat.

"*We're* on our way back," I said.

"Come on." He turned sharply, adjusting our direction.

"That's not the way to the cottage."

"My wagon is this way. Unless you'd rather walk."

I frowned. "What are you doing all the way out here? I thought you were picking up seed to take home."

"Had to drop some off at my uncle's first."

I remembered how long he'd said his days were; rescuing us was almost certainly the last thing he wanted to be doing. *We hadn't needed rescuing.* I wanted to believe it, but truthfully, I was relieved we had a ride, especially with Elodie limping like she was.

As we set off, she introduced herself. I used the distraction to snap a few branches off a nearby boxwood and stick them in the bucket, hoping the leaves would hide the Chou. Not that there was any point to keeping it secret now. I suspected Ignace already knew exactly what I was hiding. But even if he didn't, word would get out soon enough.

He and Elodie exchanged niceties, and then he turned back to me. "You seem to have a knack for getting lost."

"We weren't lost."

"Then you have a knack for wandering the woods looking as though you've been mauled by a bear. At least you didn't bring your sister along this time."

My brows drew together before I realized he was talking about the Chou I'd told him was my napping sister back when I rode in his wagon.

"Your sister?" Elodie asked.

"Never mind." I gave her a wide-eyed look, hoping she'd know it meant to keep quiet.

"What's in the bucket?" Ignace asked, his voice a touch too casual for my liking.

"Oh, um—" My mind went blank.

"Berries," Elodie said.

He rubbed his stomach. "I wouldn't mind a few berries."

I jutted my chin in the air. "We didn't find as many as we hoped. The cook needs every last one for her pies."

"I'd hate for you to disappoint the cook on my account."

I couldn't tell if he was toying with me about the Chou or upset that we had a cook. I marched on in silence.

Elodie tried to hide her ever-worsening limp as we walked up and down several small hills.

"Where is this wagon of yours?" I asked.

"Not much farther." His voice held a note of uncertainty.

"How far is that?"

He dropped his chin and mumbled, "I actually thought we'd be there by now."

I risked a glance into the bucket. The Chou remained wilted and green. I forced myself to take deep breaths, trying to remain calm. "Are you saying we're lost?"

"We're not *lost*. I'm a little turned around is all. My wagon has to be here somewhere."

My stomach writhed like an earthworm pulled from the soil.

We stepped into a clearing. An old shed crouched next to us, partially guarded from the sun by the long branches of a weeping beech tree. It was in only slightly better shape than the shack where we'd stayed the night. Moss grew across its roof.

Ignace puffed his cheeks and blew out a mouthful of air.

"You have no idea where we are, do you?" I asked.

He adjusted his tunic. "I definitely didn't pass this on the way here."

I blinked back tears. "I can't believe this is happening."

His gaze shifted from the shed to my bucket. A look I couldn't read crossed his face. He chewed on his lip.

My fist squeezed around the handle.

He nodded as if he'd made a decision, then he pulled open the door to the shed and poked his head inside. "It's a bit cooler in here. Why don't you two rest and I'll go find the wagon."

Elodie and I exchanged unhappy glances. We couldn't afford to stop. But Elodie was in tremendous pain and there was no point trekking about the woods if we'd lost our way.

"Fine," I said, stepping inside.

Elodie followed.

I continued. "But you'd better—"

The door slammed behind us. I whirled around

in time to hear a lock slide on the other side. Elodie pushed on the door. It didn't budge.

"Open the door!" I yelled, pressing my eye to a crack.

Ignace stood with his hands over his mouth as if he couldn't believe what he'd done.

"Let us out!"

He began pacing.

"What are you doing?"

He whirled toward the door. "Where'd you get the Chou?"

I squeezed the bucket to my chest. "What Chou?"

"For rabbits' sake," he said, running a hand over his head. "I saw the Chou when you fell asleep in the wagon."

"That doesn't mean you have the right to *kidnap* us."

"I didn't—it's not like I planned this." He resumed pacing. "You have everything you want in life and then some. Why should you be the one to discover the Warren? It isn't fair."

"I didn't discover anything. I found the Chou in the woods."

"Let me get this straight. You happen to find a

Chou in the woods and right after that, we start having problems with deliveries, and I'm supposed to believe it's coincidence? Just because I don't go to your fancy school doesn't mean I'm stupid."

"I'm not saying you're stupid. But I don't know where the Warren is. Come on, let us go."

"So you can run back to your maman and tell her what I've done?"

Elodie yelled through the door. "Maybe we can make a trade."

She elbowed me.

"The only thing I have on me is my ring, but it's yours if you want it. Or we can send word to my maman. She'll give you anything you ask for."

"And the moment she has you back, she'll take everything away." His shoulders slumped as he wiped a bead of sweat from his face.

"It's not too late. You can still let us out. We can pretend none of this ever happened."

His eyes held only sadness. "Easy for you to say. You'll go back to your comfortable house, your comfortable life. What about me? Don't you see— this is it. This is my chance to change everything. I need you to tell me where the Warren is."

"I told you. I don't know."

"I don't believe you." The dry grass crunched as he paced back and forth.

I rested my head against the door. "What do you want the Warren for, anyway?"

"Chou would be worth a lot more than wheat or lentils," he said. "If I'm going to be stuck farming the rest of my life, I'd at least like to make a decent profit."

I gasped. "You can't do that!"

"Let me get this straight," he said. "You can help yourself to the Chou, but it's not all right for anyone else?"

My mouth snapped shut.

I'd only taken the Chou because I was desperate.

Wait a rabbit's breath.

I wasn't the only one being forced into a future I didn't want. "Ignace, I understand why you're doing this. I do. But I can help you figure something else out, if you'll let me."

He snorted.

I had to get through to him. "This Chou is sick. If we don't get it help, the baby will die."

The footsteps stopped. "Sick how?"

"It's starting to wilt. I'm afraid it's going into shock. I don't know how much time it has left."

The footsteps resumed. "That's not my problem. If you want to save the Chou, I'd suggest you start thinking about the location of that Warren."

He wanted us to think he didn't care, but his voice shook.

Maman always said a leader should encourage her population to embrace the best version of themselves. I was no leader, but maybe the strategy would work.

"Ignace," I said in a softer voice, "I know you're not a bad person. You want a fair shot at life. But you're not going to get it if you let this Chou die. Please, let us out."

THWACK! The door rattled like he'd kicked it. "This is all your fault."

I sucked in a surprised breath. "I didn't ask to be locked up."

"You were the one who said I should do something else."

Elodie jumped in. "You think we don't all want something different? You think I love being a maid? Being on call all hours of the day, never having any say in anything that happens in my life? You don't see me locking anyone up to change things, do you?"

The anger in her voice stung. I hadn't realized that working for us was so awful. Maman had always been proud of the generous compensation she provided, and she gave more time off than was typical.

But deep inside, I knew my reaction wasn't entirely fair. Maman and I had never considered the impact any of our orders might have on Elodie. And I certainly hadn't listened when she'd said she couldn't leave the city yesterday. She'd done everything I'd ever asked of her and didn't even have a properly fitting pair of shoes to show for it.

The worst part was that she was trapped—she wasn't qualified to do anything else and her family needed every penny she made. Generous compensation or not, she obviously didn't earn enough to support a family.

Crickets chirped as we waited for his response.

"I'll think about it."

His footsteps receded.

"Wait," I yelled, pounding on the door. "Don't leave us here!"

I pushed my eye up against the crack in time to see him disappear into the woods.

I sank down on the ground as Elodie checked the walls for loose boards.

"Do you think he'll come back?" she asked.

He'd given me a ride when he didn't have to. And shared his food, too. "He's stuck working on his family's farm. I don't think he means us any harm. He'll come back after he's had time to think things through."

I tried to make my voice reassuring, but the last bit came out more like a question. A trickle of sweat ran down my back.

"He doesn't look much like a farmer," Elodie said. "He's scrawnier than a carrot."

She was right—Ignace wasn't much more than skin and bones. I wouldn't have expected a farmer's kid to go hungry. I remembered the people shouting at the theater. Apparently, the whole country was starving right under my nose—under Maman's nose.

Elodie finally gave up looking for loose boards— we were stuck here until Ignace let us out. (I had to believe he'd come back to keep the panic simmering in my stomach at bay.) She sank down across from me, wincing as she peeled off her shoes. The shack didn't have any windows, but cracks let in beams of light that crisscrossed the space, highlighting the dirt floor, an empty burlap sack crumpled in the corner, and the crushed leaves Elodie had removed from her shoes.

"How bad is it?" I asked.

"Those shoes aren't going back on my feet anytime soon."

I wished I had access to our garden; I'd make her the same mixture of garlic-and-thyme-infused water our nurse had made Maman soak her feet in when she came home with a blister.

Beads of sweat balled on my forehead and rolled down my face. (It had been cooler in here when we arrived, but now the shed was like an oven.)

I moaned. "When's he going to return?"

I longed to pull the Chou from the bucket and cradle it in my arms, but I couldn't take any chances on my body heat drying out the roots even more quickly. I stroked its leaves, willing my sister to stay strong.

As the minutes passed, her movements became more frequent. I pushed the bucket to a stripe of sunlight and studied the Chou's color. No change. The slightly sour smell, like milk on the edge of spoiling, was still there, too.

The leaves rippled and bulged.

"Do you think she's all right?" Elodie asked.

Tears built up behind my eyes. Aimée was obviously in distress. I longed to peel back the leaves and cradle her in my arms, but a baby taken from an unripe Chou wouldn't have lungs strong enough to survive. "We have to do something," I whispered.

Elodie jumped up and began banging on the door. I joined her, pounding so hard my fists burned. Perhaps between the two of us, we could break it open. Minutes passed before we admitted failure. I sat, the bucket in between my crossed legs. Aimée's squirming had decreased, which worried me more than her activity earlier.

"Please," I pleaded. "Stay strong. Help will be here soon, I promise."

Elodie kneeled next to me and began singing. Her soft, sweet voice wrapped around me like a hug.

The song was about unrequited love, but it wasn't the words that captivated me. It was her voice—the emotion, the texture. The longing.

I'd heard other singers before, of course, but I'd never experienced this feeling of—of what? Of being understood. As if Elodie had burrowed her way into my chest, as if she were channeling my heartache into words.

This whole thing had started because I wanted a sibling, someone to help bear Maman's heavy expectations. But this little bundle of leaves had turned into something more.

Even though Aimée had only been part of my life for a couple of days, even though I hadn't really met her yet, it was like her roots had spread through my heart and filled the cracks.

The song changed, growing louder and more powerful—in it, I heard my own fear. My anger. If only the stupid rabbit hadn't chased me to the cottage. If only Ignace hadn't locked us up. If only the Chou wasn't spoiling. I'd always thought that nothing was worse than loneliness. That was before I had to sit silently by while someone I loved suffered.

Elodie's voice softened as the melody slowed, drawing to a close. I swiped at the tears that had flooded my eyes and dripped down my face. Something thumped outside the door. We jumped to our feet.

"Ignace?" I called.

No one answered. Elodie pressed an eye to a crack at the front. "No one's there."

Another bump sounded, this time followed by a scraping sound, as if someone was attempting to unlock the door. I finished wiping my eyes and peered through another crack. I drew in a sharp breath.

"What is it?" Elodie asked.

I pulled back from the crack. "The rabbit. It found us."

Chapter Thirteen: *Quincy*

When I finally opened my eyes, bright light streamed in through the unfamiliar burrow's entrance, revealing a cluster of mouse-pups[16] sleeping at my side. What in the . . . ? Last night's events came rushing back to me. I hopped up, taking care not to hurt the pups, and poked my head outside. *Rotten carrots!* The sun already blazed high in the sky.

Behind me, Maman Mouse began herding her children back to the nest. She'd squeaked periodically throughout the night, as if hoping her protests would chase me away. Or maybe she was fussing over her children. With only five pups, she had

---

16. *Technically they were pinkies, since they hadn't yet grown any fur. But by that time I'd grown accustomed to thinking of them as pups.*

plenty of time to spoil them all.

I couldn't help but think of my own maman. She did her best to carve out time for each of us, but there was always some drama that needed her attention. My whiskers quivered, but this was no time to drown in self-pity.

After checking the freshly cleansed air for any scent of danger, I glanced back at Maman Mouse one more time.

She rose up on her hind legs and squeaked. This time, it didn't feel like a lecture so much as goodbye. And maybe good luck.

I sprang from the burrow, hoping the rain hadn't washed the girls' scents away completely.

Mount Angora towered in the distance. I drew in a deep breath, stunned by its magnificence. Legend had it that an Angora Rex had once been lost in the woods. Instead of giving up, she'd hopped to the top of a nearby mountain and liked the view so much that she'd stayed there until she turned to stone. I shuddered, remembering rumors that humans on the other side of the mountain killed rabbits and carried their severed feet around for good luck. Even though it was a different country, that was one more reason not to trust humans.

I lowered my nose to the ground and detected the girls' scents almost immediately. But something didn't make sense—the smell was stronger than it had been yesterday. I sat up on my hind legs, thinking.

The girls must have gotten lost and accidentally doubled back. A faint whiff of the slightly sour Chou filled my nose.

I had to get moving. After only a short distance, the trail veered, heading away from the house. Another human scent—a male—mixed in.

My heart thundered. What if they'd arranged for a ride? Or given the Chou away?

I sped up, chased by the sun's hot rays.

Panting, I eventually burst into a meadow filled with dry, crunchy grass. On the far side, a small shack squatted under the protective branches of a gigantic tree. An incredible sound came from the shack, something like birdsong with words. Estelle had once tried to describe singing to me, but it wasn't something rabbits could do. I wanted to lose myself in the wonder—the beauty—of it.

There was no time for that. I bolted across the field.

The Chou's sour scent grew stronger.

I gulped down my panic as I searched for a way inside. The shed's door was closed and there weren't any windows. What were they doing in there, anyway? I hurried around to the front and fumbled with the handle. The singing stopped.

A shiny mechanism on the door prevented it from opening. I could reach it if I jumped, but my clumsy paws couldn't slide the bolt aside. After a few more attempts, I returned to circling the shack. A small hole under the back corner gave me an idea.

I began scooping away the dirt. My hole started small, but it grew quickly.

It was nearly big enough for me to tuck my head inside when human footsteps echoed in the meadow. I pressed myself against the shack, lifted my nose in the air, and sniffed. Someone was coming. Not any old someone—the same someone who had joined the girls on the trail earlier. There was another scent, too—also human. Female.

I pressed myself flatter against the shack, my heart thumping like the foot of an agitated Angora Rex. If they opened the shack, this would be it—my chance to rescue the Chou. I could only hope I wasn't too late.

Chapter Fourteen: *Fleurine*

Skunk fumbled at the front door and then moved to the back of the shed and started digging. I pressed my eye to a crack in one wall, and then another, and then another, searching for signs that it had brought a rabbit army back with it. The meadow appeared to be empty.

What did it think it was going to accomplish on its own? Together, Elodie and I could handle a single rabbit, and it couldn't possibly believe I'd turn over my sister willingly.

But maybe the rabbit was on to something—maybe we could dig our way out of here. I was about to drop down to my knees when the digging stopped.

Footsteps approached the front of the shack. *Ignace!*

A woman walked next to him. She was small and stooped, her white hair thin and wispy. He seemed to be holding her hand—leading her. As they moved closer, I saw that her blue eyes were watery and sightless.

Ignace slid the bolt aside and opened the door, flooding the shed with sunlight.

I squinted at the newcomer. "Who are you?"

"An old lady who'd like to get back to her peace and quiet." Her body might be worn and wrinkled, but her voice had plenty of spirit.

"Madame Lavigne is a Chou bonne," Ignace said.

I gasped. "What—how did you find a Chou bonne? I thought you didn't even know where your wagon was?"

"The road isn't far beyond the clearing. Once I got my bearings, the wagon was easy to find."

"And her?" I jerked my chin toward the Chou bonne.

"You said the Chou was sick. Madame Lavigne harvested all of my uncle's kids, so I figured she could help."

Hope swelled inside me, along with a fair bit of

relief. I'd been right about him—he cared more than he let on.

"If you two are planning to talk me to death, you're well on your way," Madame Lavigne said. "Now where's this Chou?"

"It's in a bucket, here." I guided one of her hands toward the plant. Her wrists were small and her skin paper-thin but soft. She smelled of mint and ginger.

She pressed her palms carefully over the Chou as if gauging its overall size. She trailed her fingers down the Chou's roots. Bending until her nose touched the leaves, she sniffed deeply. Then she straightened. "How long since it's been in the ground?"

"Only this afternoon. But it's been transplanted at least twice."

"How long since it was delivered?"

I bit my lip. The last thing I wanted to do was admit that I'd been in the Warren.

"Mmmm," she said, acting as though I'd answered. "I assume no droppings have been mixed in?"

"There's still some fertilizer around the roots."

"No rabbit droppings?"

"Rabbit droppings?"

She ignored my confusion. "How long did you say you've had this Chou?"

I answered reluctantly. "Two days."

She rubbed her chin. "Have there been *any* signs of ripening?"

I shook my head, then realized that didn't do any good. "None."

Madame Lavigne's already wrinkled forehead developed a new set of creases.

"What is it?" My lungs suddenly felt too big for my chest.

"Every Chou I've ever tended has been left behind with rabbit droppings that dissolve into the soil with a good watering."

My lungs deflated as if they were fallen sponge cakes. I gasped for breath. "Please! There has to be something you can do."

"I'm a Chou bonne, not a miracle worker."

I swayed slightly, feeling as though I might faint.

A movement outside caught my eye. Skunk!

I rushed out the door, bucket in hand.

"Where are you going?" Ignace shouted, chasing after me. Elodie followed, guiding Madame Lavigne.

It took a moment for my eyes to adjust to the bright light. As soon as they did, I spotted Skunk crouched against the shed. Despite my close proximity, the rabbit was still blurry and hardly visible. I held out the bucket. "Can you help?"

Skunk's ears twitched.

"Who are you talking to?" Ignace asked.

"Hush," Madame Lavigne said.

Blurry or not, there was no mistaking the rabbit's gaunt frame. I had no idea how a rabbit could be starving when there was so much greenery around for the taking, but I lowered myself to one knee, plucked a handful of grass, and held it out with my palm open, hoping to earn his trust. (I also had no idea how to tell a boy rabbit from a girl, but now that I was this close, something told me it was a boy.)

"Here you go, little guy," I said. "Looks like you could use a good meal."

Skunk didn't move.

I spoke in my most soothing voice. "I won't hurt you. We both want the same thing—for this Chou to ripen. Have a little lunch, and then maybe you'll feel like sharing some droppings."

I inched closer.

Skunk pressed himself against the shed.

I tickled his chin with the greens, hoping he'd take a nibble.

He stood on his hind legs and used his front paws to push open his pouch.

"No," I said, dropping the grass. I rose to my feet and clutched the bucket to my chest. "There has to be some other way. I'll get you anything you want. More grass. Clover. A bundle of purple carrots. A *wagon* full of purple carrots. Anything you want. Please, help me."

His nose wiggled. His whiskers twitched.

My chest felt like it was filled with angry hornets. I wanted to yell. To scream. To ask why he was doing this. That's when the truth hit me. The rabbit wasn't the one who caused all this trouble. I mean, sure, Skunk had stolen the seeds. But no one had forced me to follow him. To take the Chou. To keep her a secret.

My legs threatened to buckle under me. My face burned with shame. I'd been so certain the rabbit was the problem. And then Ignace.

The baby kicked, making a wilted leaf bulge. The

bright sunlight revealed what I hadn't seen in the shed; the edge of the leaf was coated in slime, like lettuce gone bad. My breath caught. I'd known my sister was in trouble, but now I had to face the truth: she was dying, and it was all because of me.

Because I'd been so focused on what I wanted, on what I needed, that I hadn't stopped to think about anyone else. Not even the sister I claimed to love. The sister I'd taken—stolen—and dragged all over the country. The sister I'd planted and replanted, obviously sending her into shock.

And now here I was, wasting precious moments that could be used to save her life, begging to keep her for myself.

Fat tears dripped down my cheeks, wetting the Chou.

"Go on, child," Madame Lavigne said. "Do what needs to be done."

I closed my eyes and gathered my courage. Even though my mind knew I was doing the right thing, I had to force my body to kneel next to Skunk. A sharp rock dug into my knee.

I set down the bucket, carefully lifted the Chou,

and cradled it to my chest, resting my cheek against the soft leaves. Although the Chou didn't move on the outside, a warm ribbon of energy spread up my arms and wrapped itself around me, a silent sister-hug I could feel as surely as if her arms were around my neck.

A songbird's sweet lullaby filled the air.

"Aimée," I said softly, "I don't know if you can hear me, but you're going to be all right. This rabbit is going to help you ripen and find a family. I promise."

I remembered the Toussaints. They would be good parents—kind and loving. But the thought of my sister joining another family made my chest feel like it was cracking wide open, like I was about to drown in a river of sorrow.

"Goodbye, my petite Chou." I choked on a sob as I tucked the Chou's roots inside Skunk's pouch and then pulled it farther open to insert the Chou.

Uh-oh.

"It doesn't fit," Elodie gasped.

She was right—the plant was too large.

Skunk realized it the same time I did. He dropped his head and hopped backward. I tugged the roots from his pouch and cradled the Chou to my chest.

Standing at a window on the top floor of the cottage, I'd once watched a tornado rip through the countryside, a whirling funnel that tore up trees and destroyed everything in its path. My insides felt as if that tornado was heading straight toward us now.

"You have to take me back to the Warren," I said.

Skunk's nose twitched. Even if he couldn't understand my words, he had to know this was the only choice left. Even if I managed to find the general area the Warren was in again, there was little-to-no chance that I'd recognize which two trees were the entrance. And judging by how the tunnel had closed behind me when I'd first stepped inside and then disappeared entirely when I'd tried to find it again later, I might not be able to enter the Warren without a rabbit anyway.

Ignace cocked his head.

Leading *him* to the Warren was the last thing I wanted to do. Besides, I couldn't see how we'd make it in time if we had Madame Lavigne slowing us down.

As if reading my thoughts, she spoke up. "This old lady needs a ride home."

"Please," I begged Ignace.

He studied me, then Skunk. Emotions flitted across his face. Anger. Regret. Sadness.

When Elodie and I stood up to him earlier, I'd only managed to rile him, but I had to try again. I stroked the Chou with my thumb. "You and I are more alike than you might think. We both made decisions we aren't proud of. But it's not too late for either of us. We can still choose a different path."

His nostrils flared. "We're nothing alike," he snapped. "You have the whole country at your feet. The only thing I have to look forward to is an entire life working a plot of land I'll never even own."

I'd made things worse again. I peeked at the Chou, worried about the time we were wasting. I tried to remember everything Maman had taught me. Speak clearly. Project confidence. Give your audience hope. I didn't know if I could do any of that, but it didn't matter, because it seemed to me that in all of Maman's leadership lessons, she'd left out the most important thing—to care about *everybody*, not only the ones with influence.

Maman constantly surrounded herself with her patrons from the wealthy upper class. She wanted to do right by the country, but she wasn't willing to leave the comforts of her privileged life to do it. There was a reason we never visited the neighborhoods around the crematorium. Why Maman didn't meet with the protestors at the theater's opening. Why I never knew how hard other people had it until I met Ignace and got to know Elodie. It was easy to pretend everything was perfect when we never had to look someone who was struggling in the eye.

"You're right," I said softly.

He startled, obviously stunned by my admission.

"I'll never go hungry. I'll never be forced to spend long days working out in the fields." I looked back at Elodie. "I'll never have to worry about losing my job because I said or did something wrong. About how to feed my family."

I turned back to Ignace. "That doesn't mean we're not anything alike. The truth is, I'm trapped, too."

His eyes widened in surprise.

"I'd give anything to study botany. To start an académie of science." I hugged the Chou. "I'll never have the chance to do either."

Speaking the words out loud made my chest ache

like someone had reached their fist in and pulled my heart out. But it was time I faced the truth. No amount of wanting in the world would change Maman's mind. My chin trembled as I fought back tears.

Ignace clenched his fists. "The future Grande Lumière wants my pity?"

I shook my head, frustrated that I couldn't find the right words to bridge the space between us. The Chou kicked. "I don't want your pity—I don't deserve it. Even the worst version of my future will be easier than yours."

I stepped closer to him.

"My point is that we both need to learn that our lives probably aren't going to unfold the way we want them to. That doesn't give us the right to act like we're the only ones hurting, like our actions don't matter. I never should have stolen the Chou, and you never should have locked us up."

My eyes blurred as desperation bubbled from inside me like water from a fountain.

"We can still save this baby. Please."

He gripped the belt he wore wrapped around his

tunic. The whole meadow seemed to fall silent as we waited for his decision.

Madame Lavigne sneezed, breaking the spell.

"Blessings," we all murmured.

"You'd better get moving," Ignace finally said.

"Good boy." Madame Lavigne offered a gap-toothed smile as she held out her arm. Reluctantly, he took it.

I breathed a sigh of relief. But Elodie's feet were still bare. Raw, oozing blisters had formed on her toes.

"There's one more thing," I said.

Ignace raised his eyebrows.

"I need you to drop Elodie at the cottage."

"What? No!" She stepped closer. "I'm not leaving you!"

"I couldn't have gotten this far without you, but right now, you need to look after your feet."

Elodie looked back and forth from me to Ignace, her face crinkled with alarm. I hoped I wasn't going to have to convince her, too, because my brain suddenly felt as empty as a barren field.

"Fine." She turned to Ignace and folded her arms. "But I don't trust you one bit."

Ignace flushed.

She continued. "If you so much as look at me the wrong way, you're going to find out what us city girls are made of."

I was too devastated to manage a smile, but I liked this new, fiery Elodie better than the "yes, Miss" Elodie I was used to.

"Let's go," Madame Lavigne said. "I'm not getting any younger."

Elodie surprised me with a quick hug. I hugged her back, taking care not to let Ignace hear as I whispered in her ear.

She nodded, showing she understood.

As they made their way across the meadow and disappeared into the trees, I nestled the Chou back into the bucket. Skunk started for the woods. After a few hops, he stopped to make sure I was coming.

The bucket's metal handle pressed into my bruised palm. I'd already been forced to say goodbye to Aimée once—I wasn't sure I could bear to do it again.

My gold ring glinted in the sunlight. It'd always been a weight pulling me down, holding me back. But maybe it was something more—maybe it was a reminder of who I was, of the long line of d'Aubigné women that had come before me.

I set my jaw. Maman had raised me to be strong. To do what needed to be done.

Right now, I had a sister to save.

Chapter Fifteen: *Quincy*

I considered offering up some droppings, but I wasn't certain that I'd eaten enough recently to be of service, and I'd already suffered plenty of humiliation for one day. Besides, the moment she got what she wanted, Fleurine would take the Chou and run. The risk was too great—at this point, nothing short of the Warren's magic could restore the Chou's health.

I thumped my foot, not bothering to hide my impatience as Fleurine bid the other humans farewell. Finally, we set off. My excellent memory made navigating back to the tunnel where I'd said goodbye to Durrell as easy as carrot pie.[17]

---

17. *An expression I'd never really understood, since we didn't have pie; it was apparently based on all the strange things humans did to their food.*

Unfortunately, Fleurine had to skirt all the briar patches I could pass under, slowing our progress significantly. Darkness was tucking in around us when we finally reached the entrance, making me wonder what we'd find when we got back to the Warren. I couldn't help but hope that maybe Durrell had been wrong about the strike, that maybe it wouldn't start tonight, after all.

I ducked inside.

Fleurine waved off a bee, plucked several stems of tempest's lace from a nearby bush, and tucked them in her pocket. (I didn't know what in the whiskers that was about, but there was no time to sit around wondering.)

I held my breath as she hunched and entered the tunnel, only releasing it when she was safely inside. The entrance disappeared and darkness closed in around us. The air turned damp and earthy. I padded softly along the hard-packed path, fretting when we didn't run into a single transport rabbit.

Fleurine bumbled along behind me, her footfalls echoing in the empty tunnel. The Committee wouldn't be happy about her return, but she already knew the Warren's location—surely it was better to save the Chou than incur Great Maman Rabbit's wrath.

By the time we arrived at the Warren's entrance, it was closer to dawn than dusk. The moon was full, and bright stars twinkled in the night sky. We stepped through the evergreens, and I breathed in the sweet, milk-scented air, grateful to be home.

Four transport rabbits—obviously posted for security—greeted me. My ears drooped. So much for Durrell being wrong about the strike.

The rabbits gasped when they saw Fleurine.

"A human!" one said.

"What's she doing here?" another asked.

A third rabbit thumped his foot, calling for backup.

Within a few twitches, we were surrounded by dozens of rabbits all raised on their back legs, ready to box. Their feet drummed the ground, filling the air with agitation. Fleurine's eyes widened. Her nostrils flared. She couldn't see us at night outside the Warren, but in here we were perfectly visible by the light of the moon. The rabbits might not be as large as she was, but she couldn't hope to fight them all off if they attacked.

"What's the meaning of this?" Chesney's voice rose up over the ruckus. The drumming stopped. He pushed his way to the front and spotted me. "You're back."

Fosette and the rest of the Committee joined him. Their noses twitched.

Chesney's ears lay flat. "With a human."

"We brought back the missing Chou," I said.

The air was thick with the scent of rot. Chesney sniffed, then issued orders to Dion and another transport rabbit. Their whiskers quivered as they hopped toward Fleurine, stopping slightly out of her reach.

"It's okay," I said. "She won't hurt you."

"Says you," Dion muttered under his breath.

"Go on," Chesney said.

Dion hopped closer. He gasped, undoubtedly shocked by the horrifying state of the Chou, then rose up on his muscular gray legs and pulled open his pouch.

Fleurine settled the Chou inside. Tears leaked from her eyes. "Please, take good care of her."

Dion looked to Chesney, who nodded toward the field. "You know what to do."

Fleurine choked back a sob as Dion scampered off with a small entourage.[18]

I breathed an enormous sigh of relief.

Chesney turned to me, his ears still flat. "You brought a human into our Warren."

"Yes, but—"

"That's strictly forbidden."

"I had to," I said, desperate to make him understand. "The Chou wouldn't fit in my pouch."

"And the first time?"

"That was an accident, I swear!"

"What will happen to him?" someone asked.

"Punish him!" someone else yelled.

No, wait, what? They couldn't punish me! I'd rescued the Chou, exactly like they wanted. Like Great Maman Rabbit would want.

"Quincy!" a familiar voice yelled.

The crowd parted. "Quincy, you're back," Maman cried. "I've been worried out of my mind. Where have you been? What have you—"

---

18. *In other words, he didn't go alone.*

Seeing Fleurine, Maman fell silent. She rested her forehead against mine and trembled.

"What have you done?" she whispered.

"Banish him," someone yelled.

"Lock him up, along with the girl," someone else suggested. Ruckus broke out as everyone voiced their opinions.

Fosette sat up and thumped her foot, calling for quiet. "This girl threatens our very survival." She cleared her throat. "Finding our Warren once was bad enough. We can't possibly hope that she won't know our exact location after this second visit. We can't let her go—it's too risky."

I gasped. "You can't mean to keep her?"

Chesney's nose twitched as if he didn't like the idea any more than I did.

Fleurine's gaze darted around, as if she was searching for an escape route. It was probably better that she couldn't hear our conversation—I had no idea how this would end.

"Lock her up! Lock her up!" the crowd chanted. Their feet drummed the earth, drowning out their voices.

Fleurine crossed her arms and squeezed them to her chest.

The transport rabbits closed in on her, pressing her toward an empty burrow.

"Wait!" she cried, her voice breaking through the noise. She dropped her hands. "I know you probably can't understand me any better than I can you—"

Of course we could understand her. I pushed through the transport rabbits until I was in front, wishing I had a way to tell her that.

She continued. "I know I made a mistake. A big one. You don't have any reason to trust me, but I'm not here to hurt you. I brought a gift as a sign of my good faith." She reached her hand in her pocket, pulled out the tempest's lace she'd gathered earlier, and held it out. I didn't move.

She pressed it closer. "Go on," she said. "Take it."

First grass, now this. It seemed impossible to believe, but she really had no idea what we ate.

Fleurine studied us. Her face twisted in confusion. "You're all starving, aren't you?"

She shook her head. "I don't understand. You

have a whole forest at your doorstep. It's almost as if you eat nothing but—"

She looked down at the tempest's lace, then back at us, and let out a gasp. Her eyes widened as her hand flew to her mouth. "That *is* all you eat, isn't it—purple carrots?"

She continued thinking out loud. "That's why you won't eat this." She dropped the tempest's lace. "Or the grass I tried to feed you earlier."

I hopped closer and nuzzled her leg.

"You poor, sweet thing." She crouched down to eye level. "I'm so sorry. I didn't know. *We* didn't know. I mean, of course we knew fewer purple carrots were being produced and the costs were rising, but we didn't know we were hurting you."

"None of this changes anything," a rabbit from the crowd yelled. "Lock her up."

The chanting resumed. *Lock her up. Lock her up.*

Thoughts pelted my mind like the hail that had fallen the night before. A few days ago, I might have joined in. Now, I wasn't so sure. This girl was greedy and selfish, but she wasn't necessarily a villain—the truth was more complicated than that. I raised my voice to break through the clamor. "I don't think she'll betray us."

The chanting continued as if I hadn't spoken. I repeated myself slightly louder.

Chesney held up a paw. The chanting stopped.

"How can you be sure?" he asked me.

I could add up how many rabbits were gathered around us, how many had white fur and how many were gray, and I could figure the ages of every rabbit in the Warren. But I didn't know how to explain something my heart told me was true.

Fleurine sank to the ground. "I know you don't have any reason to trust me," she said. "But my maman is the Grande Lumière."

She held out her hand. "See here, I have the ring to prove it. If you let me go, I'll make sure she increases the carrot deliveries. I swear."

"Sounds like a bunch of rotten carrots to me," a voice yelled.

"Does she really seem like someone who's going to hurt us?" I asked. "She's nothing more than a child."

"We can't take that chance!" another rabbit said.

Arguments broke out. Again, Chesney thumped

for silence. "Our main priority must always be the protection of the Warren."

His words were heavy with resignation. I couldn't let this happen. The Committee had never listened to me before, but somehow, I had to make them start.

I sat up. "I made a mistake. I went to the city without the Committee's permission, and I led this girl back here."

Worried they'd start chanting again, I rushed ahead. "She made a mistake, too, taking the Chou. But in the end, she did the right thing."

I smoothed my whiskers, which were twitching violently. "I regret my mistake more than anything. I'm pretty sure she does, too. You can punish us . . . imprison her, banish me, but remember, Great Maman Rabbit created us to be nurturers. Life-givers. Our job is to work in harmony with the humans, not create conflict."

I peeked at Chesney, trying to gauge if my words were making any difference. His ears were pointed forward. He gave a small nod, indicating I should go on.

I remembered the panicked conversation I'd overheard when we'd arrived at the house in the country.

"Humans have always counted on us. They were upset when we missed a couple of deliveries. When they wake up and find out *no* deliveries were made, their world is going to be turned upside down."

"Good," someone shouted. "Let them suffer."

Fleurine pulled her knees up to her chest and wrapped her arms around them, trembling. We were *all* scared. For ourselves, for our futures. That's why I'd stolen the seeds in the first place. Why they wanted to keep Fleurine now. But we couldn't let our fear turn us into enemies.

"It works both ways," I said. "We can't grow our own carrots. Without humans, we won't survive, either. That's the way it's always been. That's the way Great Maman Rabbit wants it."

Durrell pushed his way through the crowd. He'd made it back! And from the confident way he was standing, I could tell the Warren had started to heal his wound. He wasn't going to like what I was about to say, but I had to keep going.

"This girl, her name is Fleurine," I said firmly. "She's learned her lesson, and I believe she'll help us. So I say we let her go and resume our deliveries. If our

Warren is going to survive—going to thrive—it will be because we all work together, rabbits and humans alike."

I wanted to fall back down on all fours and blend into the crowd, but instead I remained upright, scanning, making sure they'd heard. Making sure they understood.

Durrell moved to my side. Silhouetted in what little was left of the moonlight, he almost could have been mistaken for one of the statues I'd seen in Mignon. "My brother's the smartest rabbit in this Warren," he said. "We should listen to him."

My heart swelled.

Maman's eyes glistened with pride, but they weren't focused on my brother. For the first time in my life, I felt bigger than an Angora Rex.

"If he's so smart, why'd he do something so stupid?" someone yelled.

Frustration bubbled inside me, but it was a fair question. I'd told myself that I wanted to save the Warren. The truth was that I'd been so busy trying to prove myself a hero that I hadn't stopped to think about how my actions might hurt others.

"Even the smartest among us have to learn the ways of the world," Chesney said thoughtfully.

The mood in the Warren shifted. It was as if Chesney's words had poked holes in everyone's hearts, letting all their fear and anger drain out.

"What about the girl?" Durrell asked. "What do we do with her?"

"If she was going to expose us, she would have done it already," I said.

Chesney, Fosette, and the rest of the Committee huddled together, whispering. The Warren was so silent that we could practically hear the Chou growing.

After a lengthy discussion, the Committee turned to face us.

"Let her go," Chesney said.

I let out a deep sigh of relief. Rabbits began hopping aside, clearing a path for Fleurine to depart.

She rose to her feet and peered out at the field. The sun peeked from its burrow, illuminating Dion and his crew hovering over the sickly Chou. Fleurine raised her hand to her mouth, blew a soft kiss, and moved toward the shimmering air between the evergreens. Before she stepped through, she turned to us, dropped into a curtsey and whispered, "Thank you."

Then she disappeared into the woods.

"What are you all waiting for?" Chesney asked. "The day's not getting any younger and we have Chou to grow."

The Warren swarmed with activity as rabbits began their morning routines. An Angora Rex–sized wave of exhaustion hit me. I wanted nothing more than to stretch out and sleep, but I had to report for washing duty. I started for the burrow. We'd all be lucky to get a half carrot after last night's strike, but hopefully even a bit of breakfast would help prepare me for the day ahead. Chesney blocked my path.

Uh-oh.

But his ears were perky. "Well done, my boy," he said. "We'll make a Committee member out of you yet."

A Committee member? My mind felt like my body had when it tumbled through the river on the edge of drowning.

He continued. "Now get some rest. You're excused from washing for the day, but we'll expect you at your post tomorrow."

He hopped toward the field and started barking orders.

Maman took his place.

"What's he talking about?" I asked.

"Apparently I'm not the only one who sees your potential."

Warmth started at my chest and spread through my body. I'd spent my entire life longing to hear these words. But one thing still bothered me. "What about my ears?"

Her whiskers twitched. "The Committee has never been wrong before, and I don't expect they'll be wrong this time, either."

"You think a growth spurt is still possible?"

She laughed. "Most of the Committee members were late bloomers."

"Late bloomers?"

She shook her head. "You're so smart that sometimes I forget you're hardly more than a kitten. I'm going to have to do a better job educating you from now on."

I could hardly believe that I'd been selected by the Committee. That one day, I'd help lead the whole

Warren. While I sat trying to absorb all this new information, Maman grew serious and stuck her face right up in mine.

"Quincy, I'm proud of you," she said. "But we need to get one thing straight. Future Committee member or not, if you ever leave this Warren again without permission, I'll be the first to track you down, and when I'm done with you, you'll regret ever thinking about the human world. Do you understand me?"

"Yes, Maman. I understand."

She didn't have to worry. The human world was fascinating, but I'd seen enough to know that I'd never find anywhere I liked as much as home.

Chapter Sixteen: *Fleurine*

Leaving the Warren empty-handed was the hardest thing I'd ever done. I couldn't stop thinking of the Chou, of the sister I'd left behind. Maybe someday, knowing that I'd done the right thing would offer some comfort, but at the moment I felt empty, like one of the keepsake eggs that vendors sold at market during the Summer Festival. The eggs were dressed up in fancy designs, but that didn't change the fact that they were hollow inside.

I stumbled into the forest, only vaguely aware that night was turning into day. I don't remember much of my journey home; I wandered through the woods along roughly the same route I'd taken the first time, reached the road, and begged for a ride to Mignon from the first wagon that came along, mumbling non-sensical answers to whatever questions came my way.

I stumbled onto our street, fighting a mixture of exhaustion and nerves. A small crowd was gathered in front of our gates. As I pushed through, angry snippets about food shortages and the rabbits not delivering reached me. Several people shouted at a long row of guards, demanding to speak to Maman.

One of the guards recognized me and cracked open the gate, allowing me to slip in. It clanged shut and the crowd roared. Two guards rushed me to the salon, which was packed with Maman's conseillères and buzzing with activity. Maman paced back and forth in her dressing gown.

The room fell silent as I entered. "Fleurine!" Maman gasped.

I expected a barrage of angry questions, but instead she pulled me close and buried her face in my hair.

I stood stiffly, unsure how to respond. Maman never left her quarters without looking impeccable. And I couldn't remember the last time she'd hugged me.

"I thought I'd lost you," she whispered.

The fear in her voice unlocked everything I'd been holding inside. My body shook as I wept, releasing a storm of emotions. I cried for the sister I'd loved and lost, for the hunger that stung my belly, for the pain that throbbed in my feet—for the future that I knew awaited me.

I'd been so stupid, thinking that adding a little sister to our family could solve my problems. I'd told myself I wanted a friend, but truthfully, a tiny part of me had hoped a sister would fill Maman's shoes. As if I could have made her grow up loving the pressure, wanting to govern. I was no better than Maman, placing all my expectations on someone who didn't want it, hadn't asked for it.

My sobs turned to sniffles. The room had emptied, but Maman rang for a kerchief and tenderly wiped the tears from my face.

I pulled back and noticed that I'd gotten her dressing gown wet. "Your gown—"

Maman waved a hand dismissively. "There's always another dressing gown."

"I'm sorry," I said. "For everything."

She cradled my chin in her fingers. "You have some

explaining to do. But first you need a bath, and I suspect a good meal as well."

I had more pressing concerns. "Has Elodie—"

"I received word that she stayed the night at the cottage. She should be arriving shortly."

I breathed a huge sigh of relief. "You can't fire her," I said. "None of this was her fault, not any of it. I forced her to come along, and then the rabbit followed us, and I dragged her into the forest, and—"

"Fleurine," Maman said, holding up a hand, "that's enough for now. We'll finish this conversation when you're less . . ." She wrinkled her nose. "After you've cleaned up."

"Promise you'll hear me out."

"Later," Maman said firmly.

After I was cleaned, my feet bandaged, and my stomach fed, I slipped into the library. Though Maman had threatened to get rid of the book, *Advances in Plant Knowledge* rested on its shelf, its thick green binding and gold lettering practically calling my name.

I perched on the edge of a gilded chair and skimmed the pages, hoping for some information on how seeds might mix together. I didn't find anything like that, so

I returned to the chapter on pollen, picking up where Maman had previously forced me to leave off.

There were reports of scientists who believed not only that plants could move pollen around on themselves to create seeds, but also that bees and insects acted as a go-between from plant to plant, helping create new offspring.

I dropped the book in my lap. The theory explained everything. The seeds from tempest's lace and purple carrots hadn't literally combined—if bees really did collect and distribute pollen, then it was entirely possible that they'd created some sort of in-between plant, not fully either!

Our butler poked his bespectacled head through the door. "Your maman would like to see you."

Uh-oh. Now that Maman's initial relief had worn off, she'd want answers. My scratchy throat felt as if I'd never drunk water a day in my life, but I didn't dare keep her waiting any longer.

Though it was midafternoon, Maman was in bed, still in a dressing gown, her hair tangled about her shoulders. She patted the coverlet.

I settled beside her and twisted my ring.

"Madame Faucon sent word from the cottage that you and Elodie had shown up but then disappeared. I was out of my mind with worry."

"I know. I'm sorry." I hung my head, then lifted it.

"Did—" I was pretty sure I knew the answer, but I had to ask. "Did the rabbits make any deliveries last night?"

Maman's jasmine perfume wafted toward me. She frowned. "Not a single one. Are you telling me you had something to do with that?"

Slowly, haltingly, I told her about the rabbit, about the Warren, about the Chou I'd come to think of as my sister. About my efforts to help it ripen, about giving it up. I didn't dare look up while I talked, too afraid to see the disappointment etched on her face. (I didn't mention how the rabbits were starving or my theories about how we might help them—I figured that would be one carrot too many for Maman at the moment.)

When I finished, I braced myself for her response.

"You did all this because of me?" she finally asked.

I swallowed. "It wasn't because of you, exactly," I said, not wanting to hurt her feelings. "It was only—"

"The pressure I put on you." She folded her hands together. Her knuckles turned white.

"Maman," I said, searching for something to say to fix the problem.

"Did you know that when I was your age, I didn't want to become the Grande Lumière, either?"

"What?" I couldn't believe I didn't know this.

"I wanted to be a ballerina." She gave a small laugh. "Imagine it, me spending my life twirling across a stage."

"What happened?" I tried to picture Maman as a dancer.

"I showed some early promise, but I never rose to the top of my class. Eventually, I started taking fewer and fewer lessons. As I got more involved in helping Maman, I realized leadership was something I was really good at."

"But Maman—"

"I won't make excuses for myself and you shouldn't, either. I thought you were like me, that you'd come around. I had no idea how much you hated the idea. How much pressure you felt."

I bowed my head. I *had* always felt pressured, but

I'd also assumed that leading the country was something I'd be terrible at. That Maman was born knowing how to do it. The last few days had taught me that maybe it was something that could be practiced—learned. That maybe someday, I could be good at it, too.

Maman continued. "My goal was to prepare you for the challenges you'd face, the burdens you'd carry. But I should have gone about it differently. I see that now."

"Does this mean—"

"I'll have to think about your place at the Académie of Leadership."

Relief loosened the tight knot in my chest. Even if leadership could be learned, I didn't want to study it day in and day out. "Thank you, Maman."

"Fleurine, this changes nothing long term. Our family has a responsibility to the country. To the people."

A few days earlier, the idea of becoming the Grande Lumière filled me with dread. Now I saw how much work there was to be done, how many ways I could make a difference. I'd wanted to understand the purple carrots to gain a sister, but if we could unlock the secrets of their reproduction, the other applications could be limitless. We could increase crop yields for all kinds of food, improve their drought resistance—lower food prices. I remembered the hungry protestors at the theater and the crowd outside our house. The conversation I'd had with Elodie.

"Maman," I said hesitantly.

"Oui?"

"Did you know—do you know about Elodie's family?"

She tilted her head. "In what sense?"

"Her maman is sick. Elodie's wages are supporting them."

"That may be, but they receive baskets every week."

"They don't. Not since Elodie turned twelve."

Maman shifted and cleared her throat. "Yes, well, I suppose that's true. If she's twelve . . . We can't support their family forever."

"You knew about this?"

"Not about her family specifically, no. But our resources aren't unlimited. There have to be restrictions, otherwise no one would work, ever."

I thought of what I knew of Elodie. Of Ignace. They weren't looking for handouts.

"Maman," I said, "people are hungry. And it's not because they're lazy or trying to take advantage of the system. It's because things are changing. You said it yourself—"

"The Grande Maman in the Moon—"

I felt badly for interrupting, but I needed to finish. "I know we owe everything to the Grande Maman in the Moon, but she chose our family for a reason. Because she knew that we'd do right by her people. They're hurting. Maybe the Grande Maman didn't plan for people to flock to the cities, or food and purple carrot prices to shoot up, or the rabbits to starve. Or perhaps—"

Maman held up a hand. "The rabbits are starving?"

I'd forgotten that I'd left that part out. "The statues around the city make the rabbits seem large and plump. But they only eat purple carrots."

Her eyebrows pulled together. She didn't get it.

"With the prices of purple carrots increasing, we're requesting fewer babies. That means fewer purple carrots for the rabbits. You should see them—they're hardly more than skin and bones."

Maman rubbed her forehead. "I can't believe I didn't think of this."

"How could you have? A decrease in babies wouldn't be obvious to us—not like it would be to the rabbits. People are flocking to the city, making it seem as though there are more children than ever. Besides, we couldn't have known that the Angora Roux's diet was so different from other rabbits."

Maman adjusted the thin gold bracelets that graced her wrist and fretted. "I could order an increase in the number of carrots per bundle, but then there'd be even fewer families requesting babies. And that does nothing to solve the food shortage."

I sensed an opening. "I think I can help."

"Fleurine, this a matter for me and my conseillères."

"That's not fair!"

Maman frowned.

I tried again, this time carefully moderating my voice. "You've spent my entire life training me to become the next Grande Lumière. But times are changing, and the country is changing. Surely, the Grande Maman in the Moon wants us to change along with it? To help our people, and the rabbits, in every way we know how? Please, Maman, you *have* to let me try."

She sat in stunned silence. To be honest, I was rather stunned myself. I had no idea how much had been stewing inside of me. I plowed ahead, explaining my theory about the purple carrots mixing with tempest's lace. "If I'm right, we should be able to cross plants that we know actually produce purple carrots to get unaltered seeds and increase purple carrot production relatively quickly."

"I don't know," Maman said.

"This wouldn't only fix purple carrots—we could work on crops of all kinds." I rushed to correct myself. "Of *most* kinds, anyway." Before all of this started, I'd hoped to unlock the secrets of even the Chou.

But now that I'd been to the Warren, now that I'd met the rabbits and saw their suffering, I understood that their survival depended on our actions. Even though we hadn't meant to hurt them, we had to make sure we didn't do it again.

I studied the vase of blooming flowers on Maman's dressing table. A small sprig of tempest's lace peeked out from the middle. Despite their appeal, they would have to be carefully managed so as not to further upset the natural order.

Maybe that was true of all my scientific endeavors. I felt certain that we could improve the rabbits' lives by controlling the spread of tempest's lace and increasing the purple carrot supply, but if the Grande Maman in the Moon had wanted us to grow our own Chou, she wouldn't have gifted us the rabbits in the first place.

Maman continued fussing with her bracelets.

"Please, Maman. The people, they're counting on you. The Grande Maman in the Moon is counting on you. And the rabbits are, too."

Silence stretched between us.

"When did you become so persuasive?" she finally asked.

"I had a good teacher."

Her brows furrowed, but there was no anger in her eyes, only thoughtful concern.

I nudged her. "Is that a yes?"

"It seems we have to do something."

I bounced on the bed. "I have some ideas about how to—"

Maman smiled. "There's plenty of time to think about all that. Right now, we need to get dressed, and I've got to find someone to sing tonight's anthem—our soloist has come down with a sore throat."

The Summer Festival fireworks! There'd been so much happening the last few days that I'd completely forgotten the best part of this week's celebration. I sprang from the bed, partly because I couldn't wait for the display and partly because I knew exactly who we could get to sing the anthem.

I paused before climbing into the ceremonial carriage, checking to make sure the dusky sky was clear. Luckily, there wasn't a cloud in sight.

"Hurry," Maman called from inside, where she was waiting with Mesdames Pauline and Blanchet. "We're already behind schedule."

I settled next to her. Our driver closed the door. The carriage lurched and then pulled away from the house.

After dressing, Maman had personally met with the crowd that had gathered outside the house. Now the streets were empty except for small clusters of people who had obviously gotten a late start. They were dressed in their holiday finest, their clothes brightly colored, the girls' gowns trimmed with ribbons and lace.

We passed a maman cradling an infant in her arms. My chest panged. Someday, Aimée would be harvested. Join another family. I'd never stop searching the faces of babies—and eventually children—wondering if one of them might have been my sister. It didn't seem fair, but apparently the right choices in life were sometimes the ones that caused the most pain.

"I've been thinking," Maman said, interrupting my thoughts.

She was using her serious voice, the one that warned me to pay careful attention. I folded my hands in my lap and sat up as straight as possible. "Yes, Maman?"

"If our actions have in any way harmed the rabbits, even unintentionally, then we have an obligation to fix the problem. And if there's a way to increase our food production, to improve the lives of our people, then I'd be negligent not to pursue it. I'd be equally remiss if I didn't assign our best and brightest minds to the project."

I sat up straighter.

Madame Blanchet jumped in. "But the Grande Maman in the Moon—"

Maman held up her hand. "I appreciate your counsel, but change is happening whether we welcome it or not. I've been reminded that the Grande Maman in the Moon won't be happy if we don't do our best to shepherd in the right kind of change."

Maman smoothed her skirt. "Madame Pauline, please begin making the necessary preparations for an Académie of Science."

Dimples appeared on Madame Pauline's cheeks as she accepted Maman's orders. Madame Blanchet's lips pressed into a tight line.

I threw my arms around Maman's neck. She stiffened. "There is one condition."

"Anything," I said, pulling back.

"You'll have to agree to tutoring at the Académie of Leadership once a week. Your path to becoming Grande Lumière may not be a traditional one, but I have no doubt that you'll help pull this country into the future."

A wide grin spread across my face. There was no

end to the discoveries waiting to be made. As the Grande Lumière, I'd make sure we pursued each and every one of them.

I brushed my thumb over my ring, hardly daring to believe my change in fortune. I'd thought for sure that my future was hopeless, that I was going to be forced to take a narrow, straight road leading to nothing but misery. But life was full of surprises, and instead, I'd ended up on a winding trail that led exactly where I needed to go.

The carriage pulled up to the crowd that had gathered in the Gardens.

The sweet smell of summer flowers and spun sugar greeted us as the doors opened, but the crowd's cheers were muted as Maman and I made our way onto a platform decorated with elegant ribbons and chairs for Maman's special guests. A thick cloud of worry hung in the air—word that there hadn't been any deliveries had obviously spread.

Maman surprised me by walking directly to the podium without greeting her wealthy supporters first. Unsure what to expect, I slid into my seat. After she called for silence, Maman acknowledged the lack of Chou deliveries, explained the problem, and presented a new Purple Carrot Edict requiring double the number of purple carrots in each bunch.

The crowd buzzed, frustrated by this new strain on their already stretched budgets. When Maman promised to subsidize the costs until prices came down, happy whoops and cheers rang out over a loud round of applause.

After we settled, Maman introduced the singer who would be performing tonight's anthem.

Elodie climbed the stairs to replace Maman at the front of the stage, looking resplendent in a glimmering emerald gown Maman had helped her find. After a moment's silence, she began to sing. The first few notes came out wobbly. The crowd murmured. She glanced back, her hazel eyes wide and nervous. I nodded, hoping she could see that I believed in her.

Her lips curled up in a smile. She turned back to the crowd and threw herself into Montpeyroux's national anthem. The wobbles disappeared as her voice turned strong and sure, sliding up and down and filling the air with hope and joy. After the first few lines, she used her hands to invite us all to join in. Together, we raised our voices and celebrated our country, our connections, our future.

When we finished, thunderous applause once again filled the air.

Elodie curtseyed and then took a seat at my side, her face stretched into a wide smile. I smiled, too. Her success meant that I'd lost my lady's maid, but that was fine by me, because in the process, I'd gained a friend.

More than a friend. I'd thought I had to have a sibling in order not to be alone, but now I understood that we didn't have to share the same roots to be family. Elodie had proven herself on every count; she'd even kept Ignace's involvement in everything that happened a secret. I still hadn't asked Maman for help securing him a spot on a ship, but I planned to do that first thing in the morning. (I knew I probably shouldn't trust him after what he'd done, but he wasn't the only one who'd made a snap decision without thinking through the consequences.)

The first fireworks shot into the dark, dazzling orange and blue and red streaks of light that exploded into carrots and rabbits and roses before fizzling and falling to the ground. I slid one hand into Maman's and the other into Elodie's and squeezed them both. A warm glow spread through me, working its way up each of my arms and into my heart. For the first time in as long as I could remember, my family was *Homindae perfectus*.

In Case You're Wondering . . .

Growing isn't all it's cracked up to be. Though my siblings' snores fill the burrow, a terrible pain in my left ear ensures that I'm awake when Durrell returns after a long night of deliveries. (My body is as puny as ever, but my ears are now the largest in the Warren and show no signs of stopping.)

"Good evening, greetings, good night," I whisper grumpily.

Durrell returns my greeting. There's enough moonlight for me to make out a bundle of fat carrots in his bulging pouch. He adds them to the already overflowing pile at the back of the burrow and frets. "Half of these are going to rot before we have a chance to eat them."

Fleurine kept her word—our carrot supply more than doubled as soon as she left the Warren. Not only that, but the humans have been working some kind of magic, and the size of the carrots has been steadily increasing. We can't complain about our full bellies and gleaming coats, but the heavy loads are exhausting the transport rabbits, and we're running out of storage space in the burrows.

"You've got to talk to the Committee," Durrell says.

I lift one ear. "And tell them what?"

"I don't know—maybe we need to stop taking every carrot the humans leave for us. Or maybe someone should see if the girl can help?"

My bad mood falls away, and my whiskers quiver with excitement. Though the Committee has kept a careful eye on Fleurine in the two years since she left, there hasn't been any contact. Perhaps I could be an ambassador?

I rub my aching ear. "I'll see what I can do."

(Now that I've been promoted to a Committee member-in-training, they actually listen to me—at least some of the time.)

Durrell bites into a crunchy carrot.

"Pipe down," Estelle mumbles. "Or I'll pummel you both."

Sophie sits up and licks a paw. "What's happening?"

"Nothing," Durrell and I say in unison.

"It's not dawn yet," I say. "Go back to sleep."

"I won't be able to sleep now," she says. "Will you tell me a story?"

Durrell groans. "So much for getting any rest."

"You're busy stuffing your face anyway." I turn to Sophie. "What do you want to hear?"

"My favorite—the one about you leaving the Warren."

My nose twitches. "I'm not sure I remember that one."

She giggles. "You tell it all the time."

"Get on with it," Durrell says. "And don't leave out the part about how your big, brave brother rescued you."

"Quincy's the real hero," Sophie says.

"Aren't you supposed to be sleeping?" Durrell nips at her playfully.

"There aren't any heroes in the story," I say firmly. "We all did what we thought had to be done."

Durrell harrumphs.

"Careful," I warn him. "Or I'll recast you as the villain."

"You wouldn't dare."

That's true, I wouldn't. But not because I was scared of him. Because no matter how much Durrell used to ruffle my fur, I know now that he'd always been on my side. And when I'd finally built up the courage to tell him that he hadn't always made me feel like it, he'd felt terrible. He's made a real effort to treat me—and all the other rabbits in the Warren—with more respect ever since.

Durrell finishes his carrot and licks his paws clean. He and Sophie stretch out on their sides. I settle into a comfortable position. "Our story begins the morning Maman rose early to sort carrots at the back of the burrow, waking me from a restless slumber."

"Don't forget the part about the fox," Sophie reminds me in a drowsy voice.

I tell the entire story, not leaving out a single detail. By the time I'm done, everyone is snoring. The cacophony of noise is music to my ears, which have finally stopped aching, and I purr[19] contentedly.

---

19. *Of course we purr. How else would we show we're happy?*

Though the Committee invited me to move into their burrow, I'm glad I declined. I might be part of the Committee by day, but at night I'm plain old Quincy Rabbit—and that's perfectly fine with me.

Author's Note

While I was writing my debut novel, *The Wolf's Curse*, I thought of it as my "death book." When it came time to choose a subject for my second book, I was lamenting to a friend that I wanted to write a companion novel focusing on birth, but the topic didn't feel appropriate for middle grade readers. She asked if I was familiar with *La fée aux choux* (*The Cabbage Fairy*), which is a silent short film first produced in France in 1896. She went on to explain that the French version of our stork mythology holds that instead of babies being delivered by storks, they come from cabbage plants. (I later learned that this actually comes from a European folktale in which boys come from cabbages and girls from roses. *rolls eyes*) As soon as the words came out of her mouth, I knew that I'd found my next book idea.

After viewing a 1900 remake of the film (the 1896 version was lost or destroyed) and learning more about its history, I was even more enamored. *La fée aux choux* was created by Alice Guy Blaché, who many believe was the first female filmmaker in the world. In addition, *La fée aux choux* is regarded by many as the first narrative film; that is, the first film to tell a story. Guy Blaché went on to become a major force in filmmaking; she and her husband established what was, at the time, the largest film studio in the United States (and one of only two owned by women).

At the same time that I realized my next story would feature babies grown in cabbage-like plants, I knew that I wanted them to be delivered by rabbits rather than fairies. This decision led me to some fascinating discoveries about rabbits. For example, did you know that rabbits don't naturally eat carrots, which are not particularly good for them due to the high sugar content? Because my story is a fantasy, I chose to take liberties with a number of rabbit facts, including their diet (making purple carrots essential to the rabbits' survival), their anatomy (to the best of my knowledge, there aren't any rabbits with pouches, and they don't have great color perception), and their life span (wild rabbits seldom live longer than a year or two).

In addition, I played with the timeline during which facts and practices established by sciences such as agriculture, botany, and taxonomy would have been known. For example, while Rudolph Jacob Camerarius is generally credited with the initial experiments exploring the idea of plant sex and pollination at the end of the 1600s, it wasn't until the mid-1700s that the role of insects in pollination was understood, and it was still more than a hundred years after that before these ideas gained widespread acceptance.

Finally, I'd also like to note that during the Renaissance, women were, for the most part, prohibited from formally studying many sciences, although there is plenty of evidence to suggest that they nevertheless played a role in advancing our understanding of botany and a variety of other fields. If you're interested in learning more about their many scientific contributions, *Women in Science: 50 Fearless Pioneers Who Changed the World*, by Rachel Ignotofsky, is a great place to start.

Acknowledgments

Writing a book during a pandemic was no easy task; where my words usually flow quickly and my first drafts are usually completed in a matter of weeks, this story took months. Without the support of my beloved friends and critique partners Julie Artz, Kami Kinard, Sue Berk Koch, Rebecca Petruck, and Eileen Schnabel I'm not sure I ever would have made it to the finish line. Thank you all for the never-ending brainstorming, friendship, and support. (A special shout-out to Julie for introducing me to *La fée aux choux* and to Rebecca for patiently reading more than one false start.)

A. J. Sass, Jennifer Brown, and anyone else I might be missing, thank you for providing early feedback on the idea. Jaiden, thank you for the careful read; I apparently owe you two ponies now? Adam, Jaiden, Sienna, Hannah, and Sam, thank you for the brainstorming sessions and creative input that wasn't always useful but led to a lot of laughter during an otherwise difficult year. Jaiden and Sienna, I'm sorry for embarrassing you by using the words "plant sex" in my book.

Sara Crowe, I owe you a wagonful of purple carrots for championing me and my work. Martha Mihalick——I owe you an Angora Rex–sized debt of gratitude for your thoughtful guidance. Without your careful eye and never-ending list of world building questions, this story might never have blossomed. Anna and Elena Balbusso——you did it again; the illustration you created for the cover is a true work of art.

Endless thanks to the entire team at Greenwillow and HarperCollins, especially to managing editor Lois Adams, art director Paul Zakris, Taylan Salvati, Emma Meyer, and the rest of the marketing and publicity team. I'd also like to thank Sarah Thomson for her copy edits, Erin Entrada Kelly (who deserves a lifetime supply of purple carrots), my debut group and street team, the entire kidlit community, and most of all, my readers. Without you, my stories would only be words on a page. Thank you.

We acknowledge the support of the Canada Council for the Arts.

Canada Council   Conseil des arts
for the Arts   du Canada